Yaosen: The Kiss

Nancy Richter

TRANSLATED BY MAX REGER

Yaosen: Der Kuss

German Original:

Editing: Alia Emma Boecker

Proofreading: Andreas Spang

Beta readers: Jas J., Jasmin B.

Yaosen: The Kiss

English Translation:

Translation: Max Reger

Proofreading: Ami Kim, TJ Jarrett, Jen Speck

Beta readers: Adele, Mel Lane, Isabel Julia Meyer, Michael Romasanta, Paige Q. Thompson

Cover Design: MyFairy

Illustrations: Art de Jey, fluffydumplin, Hatzumomo, Irularts, MyFairy, Surya Dexter, yochai_art

Yaosen Map: Vladislav Demydov

The story is fictitious. Any similarities with real people (living, dead, or undead) are purely coincidental and not intended.

Copyright © 2023 by Nancy Richter

Karl-Liebknecht-Straße 9, 04416 Markkleeberg

E-mail: nancy.richter.aupitz@gmail.com

ISBN: 9798340909305

All rights reserved. Even in extracts, reprinting, processing and redistribution by photomechanical, digital or other means and use on the Internet are only permitted with the written authorization of the author. This does not apply to short quotations.

Contents

Yaosen Map	VII
Chapter 1	1
Chapter 2	7
Chapter 3	13
Chapter 4	21
Chapter 5	30
Chapter 6	37
Chapter 7	44
Chapter 8	48
Chapter 9	56
Chapter 10	60
Chapter 11	66
Chapter 12	74

Chapter 13	80
Chapter 14	87
Chapter 15	94
Epilogue	102
Glossary	136
Characters	138
Acknowledgments	140
About the author	142

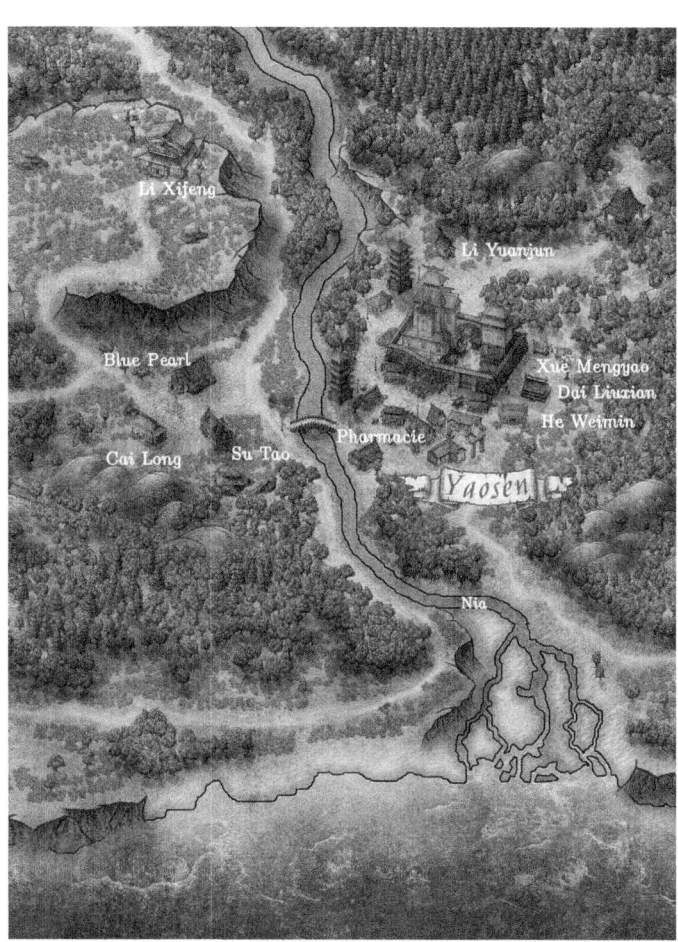

Chapter 1
Li Yuanjun

Li Yuanjun felt ashamed for what he was about to do. But only a little bit.

Crouching behind the hazelnut bush at the edge of the Yaosen forest, he felt every bit of his thirty-five years of life in his legs, perhaps some more. A mosquito's aggressive buzzing made him realize that summer wasn't over, though the days were already getting remarkably shorter.

To distract himself from the fact that he was too old for what he was about to do, Li Yuanjun focused on the sounds of the forest. Chirping birds indicated that the afternoon would soon turn into evening. Now that the daytime heat was slowly fading, a woodpecker resumed its work. The buzzing of the mosquito had stopped.

The insect had brazenly found a seat on Li Yuanjun's hand, as if it was aware of the fact that he couldn't risk being discovered by making a move. He already considered abandoning today's plans when a rustling noise in the bushes told him that his patience was about to pay off.

Only a couple of meters from his observation spot, He Weimin sneaked through the deciduous trees to disappear into the forest's darkness. Sneaking wasn't actually the correct term. He walked slowly along a barely recognizable path as if he were taking a stroll.

How He Weimin walked through the forest didn't really matter, but rather the fact that he did it at all. What encouraged the blind cultivator to go into the forest without anyone else every day for the past few weeks after finishing his work, instead of going straight to his home as he used to?

A burning pain in his hand shook Li Yuanjun away from his thoughts. The mosquito had completed its feast. If he didn't want to lose sight of He Weimin, he had to hurry.

He Weimin's long black hair, as well as the tips of his light-blue coat, had just disappeared behind one of the trees. The clothes belonged to his clan of cultivators from the west, but Li Yuanjun couldn't remember the clan's name.

Even though Li Yuanjun, unlike He Weimin, grew up in the Yaosen School of Cultivators and knew his way through the forest surrounding the Yaosen, the pursuit was a tricky task for him.

The pace and confidence with which He Weimin moved around showed Li Yuanjun that he already had to be very familiar with this area. Therefore, it wasn't just an ordinary walk—He Weimin knew exactly where he was going.

A cracking sound caused Li Yuanjun to stop. With his foot still on the treacherous branch, he listened. He Weimin's feet moved further away from him without their owner pausing. Li Yuanjun expelled the breath he had been holding. More deliberate than before, he put one foot in front of the other.

Li Yuanjun could also have asked He Weimin directly about his activities and foregone the pursuit. However, He Weimin had been avoiding him since his arrival at the Yaosen a year ago. He had skillfully evaded all conversation attempts since then. Li Yuanjun had no choice but to follow him secretly.

When Li Yuanjun peeked around a tree, he couldn't spot any sign of his prey. Nonetheless, He Weimin's very special scent caught his nose. That smell was neither flowery nor fruity, yet it always reminded him of freshly laundered bedding and cleanliness. Now, at least, Li Yuanjun knew he was close to He Weimin's heels.

Imagining what might have caused He Weimin's changed behavior made Li Yuanjun's stomach tighten.

Was the cultivator in some kind of trouble and had escaped to the Yaosen? Was someone blackmailing him? Or was he an enemy spy who wanted to pass on secret information at a hidden meeting place in the forest? By pretending to be blind, he had certainly had quite a few opportunities to obtain information.

These absurd thoughts made Li Yuanjun shake his head. Blindness could perhaps still be faked, but these serious injuries to his face and body couldn't. It was almost a miracle that He Weimin had recovered so quickly.

Li Yuanjun's heartbeat normalized until it was back in sync with the stinging in his mosquito-maltreated hand. He Weimin better have a plausible reason for his behavior.

The area Li Yuanjun was walking through seemed more and more familiar to him. Strangely, he remembered the old oak trees taller, which didn't make sense. Then he remembered that they had often played here as children. Whose idea was it back then to sneak away from class, his or Su Tao's?

They were really proud when they managed to escape the supervision of their grandmother, Li Xifeng, the Yaosen's matriarch. Back then, it had never occurred to him that Grandmother Xifeng had deliberately let them escape on occasion. Considering her experience of more than three hundred years and her extraordinary cultivation skills, it would certainly have been easy for Li Xifeng to track down her grandchildren.

Li Yuanjun's mouth became dry. That summer had been the one after his mother passed away.

When his vision blurred, Li Yuanjun almost stepped on one of those pesky branches again. Why did the forest's ground have to be littered with them? He blinked away his memories at the same time as his tears. He needed to find his way back to the present as fast as possible if he wanted to catch up with He Weimin.

He took a deep breath and wiped some sweaty red hair from his forehead, which, as usual, came loose from his plait. He listened for He Weimin's footsteps, but they had disappeared. He closed his eyes and ignored the background noise. Perhaps He Weimin had only stopped for a moment and was about to move on.

When he didn't spot any sign of life from He Weimin, Li Yuanjun tried to remember his surroundings. The path was barely recognizable anymore, yet it still had to lead somewhere.

Li Yuanjun's thoughts drifted back into the past. Back then, a ten-year-old Su Tao suggested, "Let's go to the kissing glade and scare the lovers."

This was precisely what he was looking for. Only a few hundred meters into the forest, there was a glade that teenagers, and those who had already left their teenage years, had chosen as their romantic spot.

He wondered whether the glade still existed or if it had become overgrown. When he realized that the path had to lead there, he shuddered. He Weimin could have already been on his way back while he stared into the sky, lost in memories.

Only when he had made sure that the noise of footsteps had not resumed, Li Yuanjun noticed that he had been holding his breath. He had to stop taking this matter too seriously. After all, nobody was committing any illegal activities. They had every right to be here.

Keeping this thought in mind, he straightened up as much as possible and followed the path to the glade. He didn't have to walk far until he saw the afternoon sunlight flashing through the branches. The glade was right in front of him, just behind the trees.

Li Yuanjun raised his hand to push some branches aside before he risked a cautious glance through the branches. He stopped moving. What if He Weimin had arranged a date with someone at this glade? Perhaps, every single day, he was eagerly awaited by his lover? Thinking about this, he noticed a tingling feeling between his shoulder blades.

In his mind, he thought about all the Yaosen women who could have been He Weimin's lover. But there were nothing but happy couples plus some bachelors, including himself.

Li Yuanjun was already about to breathe a sigh of relief when the inhabitants of the nearby villages crossed his mind. They were usually not averse to an affair with a male or female cultivator. His mouth became dry, and he started to feel nauseous.

He squatted down on the forest ground and took a deep breath in order to think clearly and dispel his nausea. The smell of mushrooms caught his nose, reminding him of the ongoing mushroom season. Mushrooms went with almost every single meal—as a side dish, filling, or sauce. So it wasn't too surprising that his stomach complained. It had absolutely nothing to do with He Weimin and his love life.

Happily, he wiped the sweat away from his forehead and shifted his weight back and forth on his heels. An inner voice told him to leave He Weimin and his catch in peace and return to the Yaosen. After all, Li Yuanjun wasn't ten years old any longer, so the phase of childish pranks was long gone, his inner voice warned him.

Li Yuanjun completely agreed with this voice of reason because this was exactly what it had to be. He stood up quietly and was just about to return when, despite the inner voice, he gave in and glanced through the branches. At least he wanted to take a glimpse of that woman who had managed to catch He Weimin.

The view that awaited him at the glade didn't match his expectations.

Chapter 2

He Weimin's Secret

From his observation spot, Li Yuanjun could only see parts of the glade.

The area without trees had the shape of an oval and measured probably ten by fifteen meters. Wildflowers crowded together in a shaded spot. Various tree saplings competed with each other to close the glade's gap from the edge and become a part of the forest again.

Brave, like a one-man army, He Weimin fought with his sword against the sapling's attempts. The once-green grass, meanwhile turning late-summer-brown, had been trampled down in a circle, revealing it to be He Weimin's conquest.

At least, that was how Li Yuanjun initially perceived the situation. He leaned forward a little more and saw that He Weimin was warming up for a sword fight.

Li Yuanjun stepped from one foot to the other. *So indeed, it was a secret meeting, even though, fortunately, not a date.* What was he thinking, though? An affair would be better than a fight.

Nervously, Li Yuanjun scratched his mosquito bite, but He Weimin's opponent hadn't appeared yet. Had Li Yuanjun scared him off by his presence? He Weimin showed no signs of uncertainty, moving quickly and confidently over the uneven ground. Without any sign of warning, his movements transformed into a more offensive style.

Li Yuanjun's eyes widened. What he was witnessing here was impressive. He Weimin moved with a pace that he could only dream of.

He Weimin must have been an outstanding swordsman before his blindness occurred, and judging by what Li Yuanjun could see through the leaves, he still was. Whoever He Weimin was waiting for, that someone wouldn't face an easy battle.

There was something hypnotizing about He Weimin's flowing movements. Li Yuanjun was unable to avert his gaze. When He Weimin changed to a defensive position, Li Yuanjun was so surprised that he looked around, trying to spot the possible opponent.

Nonetheless, they were still alone at the glade, which seemed certain to Li Yuanjun, because of the unchanged birds chirping and the noises of the other forest inhabitants. The two men had already become part of the forest.

The fading sun dazzled Li Yuanjun, causing him to take a few steps to the side. He had not been careful enough, though, as a crack sounded under his foot. A glance downward confirmed that he had stepped on one of the ubiquitous branches.

When Li Yuanjun looked up, he saw at the edge of his vision that He Weimin had turned toward the telltale noise, letting his sword fly.

Li Yuanjun was about to retreat when his foot got caught in the branches, making him fall to the ground. The sword remained up in the air, just a couple of centimeters in front of him, then returned to He Weimin along with a hand signal.

Before Li Yuanjun was able to show himself, He Weimin spoke up.

"You might as well come out, Li Yuanjun. It's not worth hiding anymore," he said in a gruff voice, sheathing his sword on his hip.

Li Yuanjun's clumsiness had given away his location, but how did He Weimin know it was him? The answer to this question had to wait, though. Now he had to face He Weimin, who was already waiting for a reply with a cold facial expression. He stood up, brushed the dirt off his butt, and awkwardly fixed his clothes to gain some time.

"Don't be mad at me. I certainly didn't mean to spy on you. When I was walking past the glade, I encountered you by accident," Li Yuanjun said, slowly moving toward He Weimin.

Li Yuanjun was shorter than He Weimin, but not by much. When he reached He Weimin, he was able to take a decent look at his face. The burns that had taken his vision were nothing but a slight scarring now. Unlike many blind people, He Weimin refrained from covering his eyes. To Li Yuanjun's delight, they were not milky white but rather shined golden brown in the light of the disappearing sun.

"You have beautiful brown eyes. I'm happy you're not hiding them behind a cloth," Li Yuanjun said, speaking his thoughts aloud.

He Weimin raised a hand to his face as if he wanted to touch it but then hesitated and lowered it again. "Brown eyes are nothing special. Don't distract me."

Li Yuanjun tensed up. "You can take my word for it. I was telling the truth," he lied. "I was passing by the glade purely by chance when I heard noises. Naturally, I had to make sure that everything was all right. It could have been a group of robbers, demons, or enemy warriors."

Certainly, the first two options were completely insane. He Weimin had to know that.

Robbers and thieves would have had a hard time finding anything of value at the Yaosen except for the magical weapons and artifacts that cultivators usually carried.

The last incident with the Shadow Demons of the Shawree Mountains had happened over a year ago and was settled peacefully through the efforts of two of Yaosen's senior students.

Li Yuanjun wanted to baffle He Weimin with his third assumption. However, he didn't let on and didn't make a face. He merely shook his head as if to emphasize the absurdity of Li Yuanjun's claim.

"So, you didn't reveal yourself because you thought I was conspiring with robbers, demons, or other scum?" He Weimin asked frankly.

Li Yuanjun winced at this remark, which put his conspiracy theory in a nutshell. Not knowing what to do with his hands, he scratched at the mosquito bite, which had already turned a deep red color. He was still looking for an innocuous answer when a clearing of He Weimin's throat snapped him out of his thoughts.

"I kept quiet out of concern for you." Li Yuanjun said the first thing that came to mind. "When I saw you with the sword at the glade, I figured it was better not to scare you so you wouldn't accidentally hurt yourself."

He Weimin seemed to want to cross his arms in front of his chest but then contented himself by turning his hands into fists.

"Do you really think I'm so clumsy as to injure myself during training, like one of your students?" He Weimin asked quietly.

Li Yuanjun's blood rushed to his head. He actually wanted to confuse He Weimin with his audacity, but it was by no means his intention to embarrass him.

"After seeing how skillfully you move, I don't think you should worry about it," Li Yuanjun tried to make up for his mistake. "So, you've come to the glade to practice. Why don't you join the rest of us on the training ground?"

"There is too much noise at the training ground; so, it's hard for me to focus there," He Weimin replied, lowering his head.

Li Yuanjun knew with certainty that this was a lie. He Weimin's body language was an exact copy of his students who turned up late for battle training and justified it with a silly excuse. As a teacher at Yaosen, he had seen this happen countless times. It was good to know that He Weimin was a bad liar. A smile spread across Li Yuanjun's face, which even He Weimin's next words couldn't wipe away.

"Cai Long recommended this place to me," He Weimin explained, "he said I could rest quietly here and practice the techniques that the wise Li Xifeng taught me."

Li Yuanjun hadn't missed the fact that He Weimin had emphasized the significance of *quiet*. He ignored the tinge of guilt that crept up on him.

"Did you know that this is a favorite meeting place for lovers? So don't be surprised if you get disturbed even more frequently."

He Weimin moved uneasily from one foot to the other. "You're the first person I've met here. The glade was also pretty much overgrown."

"The youths have probably long forgotten about its existence," Li Yuanjun said, gazing over the area. His initial assessment of He Weimin fighting the vegetation was not that far-fetched. He must have been the first person here in a long time.

When Li Yuanjun turned back to He Weimin, his expression had become worried. "You're not going to tell your students about the glade, are you?" he asked in an uncertain voice.

Li Yuanjun wanted to reassure He Weimin that this was not his intention but stopped himself. Over the past year, He Weimin had slowly shed his initial reticence toward others. He had even developed a deep friendship with Cai Long and Su Tao. Only with Li Yuanjun did he remain distant. All attempts to strike up a conversation with He Weimin were rigorously blocked with short answers.

Their conversation at the glade was one of the longest he had ever had with He Weimin. He couldn't let an opportunity to improve their relationship like the one he had here go to waste.

"If you insist, the glade will remain our secret," he assured He Weimin. *A secret that most members of the Yaosen share with us*, he added in his mind.

He Weimin breathed a sigh of relief, and his posture relaxed noticeably. "I really appreciate that."

Li Yuanjun felt as if he had kicked a helpless puppy. After all, it wasn't like he had planned a trip to the glade with his students. He reassured himself with the thought that it wasn't his intention to talk about the glade, so he hadn't lied.

"So it's settled. We have agreed on a secret pact," Li Yuanjun said, holding out his hand toward He Weimin. Before he could reach for He Weimin's hand, the fiery red mosquito bite on the back of his hand made him pause.

"No, that's not how it works," he murmured so quietly that He Weimin had to lean forward to hear him. "We should seal our pact properly." Satisfied with himself, he announced louder, "Have you brought anything we can toast with?"

He Weimin frowned and seemed to consider whether Li Yuanjun was serious or making fun of him. After a moment of hesitation, he sighed and said, "I have a jug of water by the trees next to the flower meadow if that meets your expectations."

This is going even better than expected, Li Yuanjun cheered himself in his mind.

"Great, my throat is already dried up. You must feel the same after your exercises. Let's not just keep standing around. We should take a seat under the trees in the shade."

At first, He Weimin hesitated, but then he nodded, apparently accepting that his training was over for the day.

When Li Yuanjun reached for He Weimin's arm to pull him toward the trees, He Weimin flinched in shocking surprise.

Chapter 3
The Pact

Li Yuanjun scolded himself for scaring He Weimin. He didn't know much about handling blind people, but even he was aware that you shouldn't abruptly touch them. And if that wasn't enough rudeness, he had also intended to drag him like a spoiled child.

"Forgive me, Weimin; I didn't mean to startle you," Li Yuanjun said while taking a step back. He thought about the best way to lead He Weimin. To his shame, he had hardly paid any attention to how others treated He Weimin when they took him across unfamiliar areas.

He Weimin had regained his composure by now. "I can walk the path alone. If you'd help me find my way a little bit, that's sufficient."

Li Yuanjun shook his head—before realizing that He Weimin wasn't able to see this gesture. "No, that's out of the question. I want to learn how to do it properly. Should we perhaps hold hands?"

Listening to these words, He Weimin's face blushed. Li Yuanjun thought He Weimin was angry at him. When he then bent his forearm, Li Yuanjun didn't know what to make of the gesture.

He Weimin said uncertainly, turning his head away, "You can lead me by the arm, holding my elbow."

Without thinking twice, Li Yuanjun hooked onto He Weimin's forearm to take some first steps together. It didn't take long until they found their rhythm.

While getting closer to the group of trees, Li Yuanjun had an absurd thought.

"Weimin, the way you and I are walking . . . this kinda reminds me of a newlywed couple on their way to their new home. To complete the picture, you only need a bridal veil, don't you think?"

These words made He Weimin stumble. But Li Yuanjun was able to hold him up by the arm.

"So it was indeed a good idea to go together after all," Li Yuanjun stated happily. "The ground is full of branches that are easy to trip over."

"Thank you," He Weimin replied.

Li Yuanjun already figured he had gone too far with his jokes when He Weimin finally answered his question.

"Oh, so you'd be the groom then, which would make me your bride."

This remark threw Li Yuanjun off balance, so now it was *he* who almost tripped. He Weimin reacted by tightening his grip on Li Yuanjun's arm, which he had only been holding loosely before.

Li Yuanjun couldn't help but laugh. "Either I'm dreaming, or you've just made a joke," it slipped out of him.

He Weimin was obviously less serious than he had thought. It was just as well for him, as this game could also be played by two.

"Agreed, I'm adaptable," he responded to He Weimin's remark. "You can be the bride for now."

He could not determine whether the trembling of He Weimin's arm was due to horror or suppressed laughter. Since He Weimin made no attempt to free himself from his grip, he decided in favor of the latter.

Li Yuanjun thought about what else he could say to cheer He Weimin up when he noticed his steps slowing down until he stopped.

"Is it possible that we're walking around in circles? When I walked around the glade by myself, it didn't seem so widespread," he turned to Li Yuanjun.

Whenever he wasn't looking at He Weimin to interpret his reactions, Li Yuanjun had been scanning the ground for tripping hazards. When he looked up, though, he realized they had circled several times around a group of trees together.

He considered the idea of giving He Weimin a hypocritical explanation as to why he had looked for the best resting spot and had to check out the surroundings very carefully. But considering he had already said enough nonsensical things today, he preferred to try the truth for once.

Blushing, which He Weimin, fortunately, couldn't see, he said, "You're right; our conversation distracted me so much that I just started walking without paying attention. When you put your mind to it, you can be a very charming conversationalist."

"Thank you?" He Weimin answered, clearly questioning. "And you're, uhm . . ."

"A chatterbox. Go ahead, don't hesitate; I'm used to others telling me that I talk first and think later. Sometimes I just talk and don't think at all."

"That's not what I was about to say. In fact, I like it when you talk a lot. As I can't recognize gestures or facial expressions, it helps me to assess the other person better."

A little bit lost, he added, "I don't know exactly where we are right now. Could you describe the surroundings to me?"

Li Yuanjun looked around without letting go of He Weimin's arm. "We're right under some trees, big ones. Next to them are wildflowers, quite pretty ones. After this dry summer, the ground is hard, and the grass looks brown. The sky . . ."

"Describing locations is not exactly your biggest strength," He Weimin said with a smile. "Better tell me where things are from my point of view so I can imagine the area."

He Weimin managed to stop Li Yuanjun from turning around in all directions, standing still with him.

Li Yuanjun took a deep breath and focused on what was important. "A flower meadow about three meters to your right. One meter to your left is a tree trunk that belongs to a group of trees growing into the glade. To your left, by your arm, there's me," he added, hoping the smile would reappear.

He Weimin shook his head yet couldn't hold back a smile. "I know where we are now. The jug of water is right by the wild orchids. May you tell me exactly where they are located?"

"I'd love to, but I don't recognize which of those flowers are orchids. You probably know their color?"

When Li Yuanjun realized that he had asked a blind man about the color of the flowers, he wanted to apologize to He Weimin, but he just laughed at him. Li Yuanjun also burst out laughing until he was in tears.

"It possibly wouldn't help you much if I described the smell of the orchids. Let's just walk a few steps toward the flowers. I'll let you know when I recognize their smell, and you keep an eye out for a jug."

IN VERY LITTLE TIME, they had found the jug, and Li Yuanjun led them back to the group of trees. These trees were oaks, as He Weimin had explained to him.

When Li Yuanjun released his arm from He Weimin, he felt disappointed. Not only was it fun to stroll around the glade with He Weimin, but it also made Li Yuanjun feel warm inside his chest.

"We can sit down," Li Yuanjun said after removing some annoying branches.

He followed his own suggestion by plopping down on the grass. He Weimin hesitated and fiddled nervously with his sleeve, from which he eventually pulled out a brown cloth. He carefully spread the cloth on the ground before sitting down on it.

"You don't like picnics, do you?" Li Yuanjun slipped out carelessly.

"I have to be extra careful because I don't know when my clothes get dirty. It's easier this way than constantly having to ask others whether I have any stains."

Li Yuanjun let his gaze wander over He Weimin's carefully embroidered clothes. In his mind, he compared his own worn clothes, which were dusty after a day of training with the students, with the precious artwork.

"You could wear brown- and green-colored clothes, then the stains would be less noticeable," he suggested.

He Weimin frowned and unconsciously ran his fingers across one of the ornaments on his clothes.

"These are my clan's colors. Replacing them with other colors wouldn't be correct," he answered, moving his hand over his mouth as if to undo what he had just said. "I didn't want to disrespect you or the Yaosen," he whispered.

"No need to hold back," Li Yuanjun reassured him. "The Yaosen school doesn't have its own color dress code. Everybody just wears what they prefer or what's available. My coat, for example, is unadorned and green-brown. The shirt is dark green, and the trousers are gray, but they were once brown a long time ago."

When Li Yuanjun noticed that He Weimin was relaxing, he reached for the jug he had placed next to him. "Now it's time for a toast to our secret pact," he announced.

Li Yuanjun swirled the jug. The content was pleasantly cool due to the place in the shade where it had been. "I didn't bring any cups," explained He Weimin, who must have heard the noise.

"Why would you?" said Li Yuanjun. "Obviously, you weren't expecting any visitors. Give me your hand. I've already opened the jug. You can drink first, then the rest is for me."

He Weimin stretched out his hand, and Li Yuanjun handed him the jug. When he hesitated to drink and looked unsure at Li Yuanjun, the latter said, "To our secret glade and that we keep it undisturbed in the future. Now drink to our pact, even if it's only with water."

He Weimin hesitantly took a sip, then, already braver, a second one. He awkwardly wiped around the opening before pointing the jug in Li Yuanjun's approximate direction. "I am not thirsty; feel free to drink the rest."

Only when Li Yuanjun had emptied the jug in a few sips did he realize how thirsty the wait and the chase had made him. He closed the jug and put it down next to He Weimin so that it could be found easily later.

Li Yuanjun leaned against the trunk of the oak tree, feeling a sense of calm and contentment coming over him. He closed his eyes and surrendered to the memories of his childhood.

"Did Cai Long tell you how the glade came into existence?" Li Yuanjun finally broke the peaceful silence.

He Weimin, who looked busy plucking out blades of grass, said, "No, but I suppose a fire caused it? Some of the older trees have bumps in their bark that you can feel."

"It was the summer I was born when the glade was created," Li Yuanjun began to explain. "My grandmother Li Xifeng told us children a story about a dragon whose breath of fire burned down part of the forest and left the bare clearing behind."

"Do you believe that?" He Weimin asked in astonishment.

"As the five-year-old I was back then, I believed every single word of it to be true. I later realized that the reason was a forest fire caused by a summer that was too dry. Grandma Xifeng wanted to use her story to show us how dangerous fire can be and encourage us to be careful."

By now, He Weimin had given up trying to keep his hands busy and had tucked them into the wide sleeves of his coat. "Your grandmother is a wise woman," he said approvingly. "A simple warning not to play with fire would probably have had the exact opposite effect."

The bird's chirpings, which had become louder without Li Yuanjun noticing, brought him back to the present. The birds had already realized for a while what he had almost overlooked. "Weimin, the sun has almost set. We should slowly make our way back if we want to get something to eat. What are you hungry for today?"

He stood up and knocked a few blades of grass off his clothes. When he saw that He Weimin had remained seated and was silent, he asked, "What's going on? Don't you want to go back to Yaosen together?"

"I'm not particularly hungry," He Weimin said with his head down, which Li Yuanjun now recognized as a lie. "Go ahead without me as long as you can still see the path. I will meditate for a while and then set off. I don't mind the darkness."

From one moment to another, He Weimin had returned to his reserved self. Li Yuanjun did not respond to He Weimin's changed behavior. He had just realized he had found the perfect excuse to spend more time with He Weimin and perhaps even create a friendship.

Chapter 4

Mushrooms

"As you wish," Li Yuanjun said, "I will be on my way now. See you at the same time tomorrow at the glade."

When he spotted He Weimin's widened eyes, he was barely able to suppress a laugh.

"Come on, we're friends now," he continued to He Weimin, whose mouth was hanging open without any words coming out. "We can work on our fighting techniques together. I'm already rusty from training with the students. What I need at the moment is to compete with an experienced fighter."

Li Yuanjun knew perfectly that he wasn't about to achieve anything by flattering He Weimin. However, he could hardly refuse him if he was doing him a favor.

He Weimin's nodding showed him that he had correctly assessed his personality. "Agreed. Let's train together tomorrow. I'd like to learn more fighting techniques from the Yaosen School."

A satisfied smile spread across Li Yuanjun's face, which, fortunately, He Weimin was unable to see.

"See you tomorrow then." Li Yuanjun said goodbye. "I'll keep some dinner for you and give it to one of the students so that he can bring it to you. You have to keep your strength up if we're going to train," he added.

Surrendering, He Weimin sighed. "Alright, see you tomorrow, and thanks for the food."

Before he finally turned to leave, Li Yuanjun couldn't resist telling He Weimin, "There are some oak trees right behind you. Three meters to your left is a carpet of white orchids, and the glade's entrance is perhaps ten meters straight ahead. And in front of you . . ."

"There's Yuanjun standing and saying goodbye," He Weimin added with one of his rare smiles.

Li Yuanjun returned with easygoing footsteps. In contrast to the outward walk, the distance back seemed very short to him. By the time he reached the Yaosen School grounds, it was already dark, while the magical lights that his grandmother maintained through her cultivation were already burning.

On the way to his house, he stopped at the Blue Pearl, the Yaosen inn, for a light meal. As he had promised, Li Yuanjun had one of He Weimin's two roommates, an older student, bring him a mushroom soup, which was the dish of the day.

As he entered the one-story house that he lived in alone, his thoughts wandered to He Weimin. Specifically, to his living situation.

Due to his blindness, Li Xifeng had placed him in a shared apartment with two of the older students. Xue Mengyao and Dai Liuxian were supposed to help He Weimin with his daily chores.

But one year after his arrival at Yaosen, He Weimin was hardly dependent on other people's help. It was time for him to move into his own place if only there were a suitable one available.

The apartment above the pharmacy, where He Weimin worked as the alchemist Deng Tingfeng's assistant, would have been perfect for him. However, it was already occupied by the alchemist, who would rather have blown up the entire building than give up his place.

All the houses were currently occupied, so He Weimin would probably have to continue to get along with his roommates for a while.

Li Yuanjun yawned profusely and ignited a magical light in the palm of his hand, which he levitated toward the ceiling. He found himself in a small anteroom that led into his living room. He rarely used the tiny kitchen for cooking, which was only separated from the living room by a curtain. The center of his home was the bedroom, which was dominated by an oversized bed. Li Yuanjun loved to stretch out in bed and hide from the cold under a pile of blankets in winter.

He placed his sword on a chest of drawers next to the door and took off his worn shoes, which landed noisily on the wooden floor. Then he went into the kitchen to make himself some tea, which he then leaned back in his favorite armchair with. As he inhaled the scent of the herbs, the smell brought back memories of He Weimin, who would surely know the exact name of these plants.

He Weimin's work at the pharmacy seemed to be paying off. Although Deng Tingfeng kept telling his customers that his assistant was only good for cleaning the test tubes, Li Yuanjun knew that this was not true. The old alchemist did not entrust his precious alchemical utensils to just anyone. He must have secretly considered He Weimin a worthy successor.

Before Li Yuanjun could fall asleep in a sitting position, he straightened up with a jerk. The teacup ended up in the sink with her twin and the dishes from breakfast. The washing up could wait until tomorrow. Li Yuanjun did some half-hearted meditation exercises before going to bed.

Li Yuanjun stretched out on his bed and quickly switched off the magic light before he could think more about the pile of unwashed laundry next to the door. Feeling warm in his stomach, which wasn't caused by the mushroom soup, along with the thoughts of tomorrow's meeting with He Weimin, he fell deeply asleep.

THE FOLLOWING DAY GREETED Li Yuanjun with fog, which slowly descended and evaporated on the ground to make way for an equally gray, cloudy sky. Although the temperatures were still mild, the typical smell of autumn was already in the air, proving to him that the power of summer had already faded.

When Li Yuanjun made his way to the Yaosen training ground, he whistled a cheerful tune, the lyrics of which he could no longer remember. The place that the members and students of the Yaosen used for training was an artificially leveled area on a plateau, overlooked only by the dwelling of the sage Li Xifeng.

Li Yuanjun watched the martial training of his students and let his gaze wander over the school grounds. Thanks to the slightly elevated position of the square, he could see the students' quarters, the forge, the Blue Pearl, some shops, the pharmacy, and his own house.

He was just about to calmly correct the leg position of one of the younger students for the hundredth time when he noticed a movement out of the corner of his eye. He Weimin had finished his work at the pharmacy and was on his way to the forest, to the glade, as Li Yuanjun knew by now. He hadn't even realized how late it already was.

The smile spreading across his face earned him an astonished look from one of his students. "Bend your left leg slightly, your right leg further outward," Li Yuanjun explained to him. "You have to repeat the movements until your body remembers them automatically. When you're in a fight, you don't have time to think about your leg position."

Later, when he declared the training session as finished, the students ran off in all directions. Did he have as much stamina at that age, too, that he still had to exert himself *after* a tiring training session? Glancing at the training ground, he made sure that nobody had forgotten anything, grabbed his sword, and headed toward the forest.

FINALLY, THE SUN HAD pushed through the clouds, which the birds cheered with loud chirping. The closer Li Yuanjun got to the forest's glade, the slower his steps became until he stopped completely. At first, he didn't know what had caused his changing mood.

He Weimin's injuries had healed completely. It was only a matter of time before he regained his fighting skills, even without his vision. Soon, there would be no reason for He Weimin to stay in the Yaosen; he would go back to his clan.

Li Yuanjun's stomach went crazy. He Weimin had just started to open up in his presence. If he wanted to make friends with He Weimin, then he had to hurry before he could disappear from his life.

He tightened up and walked the few steps that still separated him from the glade. Before he pushed his way through the branches, Li Yuanjun thought about how he should make He Weimin notice him.

"Yuanjun, you move like a herd of goats being pushed through the bushes," He Weimin greeted him first.

Li Yuanjun walked up to He Weimin, didn't really know what to do with his hands. He Weimin wouldn't be able to see a wave as a greeting. "I'm coming over to you, just stay where you are," he said instead, just so he could tell something to He Weimin to orientate himself on.

By the time Li Yuanjun had reached He Weimin, he found himself staring indecisively at the ground. What happened to his usual quick wit? It didn't suit him that his throat was tight.

"It looked like rain this morning. We're lucky that the sky has cleared up," he finally managed to say.

Li Yuanjun himself was surprised at the level of creativity he displayed. The most unimaginative, albeit most effective, way to start a conversation was to make a remark about the weather. However, since Li Yuanjun actually wanted to open a conversation and not pick up a date in a tavern, he forgave himself for his mistake.

He was just about to breathe a sigh of relief when an icy shiver ran down his spine. Had he just told a blind man that it had *looked* like rain?

"Well, at least it's not raining, visible or not," he stammered.

Without emotions, He Weimin had endured the verbal acrobatics with his hands clasped in front of his body. His body began to tremble, and he finally burst out laughing. It was the first loud laugh Li Yuanjun had ever heard from him.

"Feel free to say things like 'see you' or 'it looks like rain' to me. These are phrases that don't come across as insulting at all. As long as you talk to me and don't just make gestures, I am going to understand you. Don't overthink your words. When anything might be inappropriate, I will let you know."

Li Yuanjun tightened up, "What do we want to start with? I am sure you already did some warm-up exercises, and I've just come from training with the students, so we should be on par."

"How about some simple pair exercises that should help us to assess each other better," He Weimin suggested.

"That's what we're going to do," Li Yuanjun agreed.

After getting over some initial hindrances, they were quickly moving in harmony, with only the sound of their footsteps and the whirring of swords to be heard. He Weimin was already able to compensate for his blindness surprisingly well. He seemed to be able to spot moving things and living beings more easily than stationary objects.

Li Yuanjun would have liked to ask He Weimin about the training methods Li Xifeng must have taught him. He did not want to remind him of his blindness for no reason; he refrained from doing so for the time being. Instead, he wanted to know from He Weimin during a break, "When I observed . . . I mean, of course, when I happened to pass by here yesterday, you were reenacting a fight. What was it about?"

He Weimin stepped from one foot to the other. "That's long over, and I lost that fight. I can't find the mistake, though, and I can't keep myself from trying again and again." He Weimin's head lowered downward. By this time, Li Yuanjun knew his body language well enough to be sure that something about that story was not true.

"Maybe we should finish training for today. I have a jug of water in the same place as yesterday," He Weimin continued, sheathing his sword as if to emphasize his words.

Li Yuanjun recognized the suggestion for what it was: a diversionary tactic. He decided not to push He Weimin any further for now; he would certainly find out the truth eventually. Right now, building a friendship had a higher priority, and He Weimin had just given him the perfect excuse.

"I'm fine with that. The sun won't set for at least another hour. We still have enough time left to talk. Let's go to our oak tree together."

"Oh, so it's already *our* oak tree," He Weimin said, who had relaxed and held out his bent forearm to Li Yuanjun, just like he did yesterday.

"No need to hook me in. It's enough if you lead me by the elbow," he added uncertainly.

"That's nonsense. It's much easier this way, and we're the same height this way," Li Yuanjun replied, stowing his sword away and hooking onto He Weimin. "The oak tree is about ten meters ahead of us. We need to keep slightly to the right."

On the way to the oak tree, Li Yuanjun drew He Weimin's attention to the uneven ground and warned him about the branches on the ground. After a couple of minutes, they arrived at the oak tree.

"Is it okay if I get the jug while you make yourself comfortable?" Li Yuanjun wanted to know.

"Of course. And thank you for asking first."

While He Weimin spread his cloth on the floor, Li Yuanjun went in search of the jug. He found it in the same place as the day before, by the orchids. He saw that He Weimin had even remembered to bring two cups with him today.

Eventually, Li Yuanjun grabbed the jug and, after a moment of hesitation, the cups as well. Then he walked the few steps back to He Weimin.

He Weimin had not taken a seat, waiting for Li Yuanjun. To keep his hands busy, he fiddled with his sword sheath.

"Here I am," Li Yuanjun said, making his presence known after remembering in time that it was important to talk to He Weimin so that he would know where his counterpart was.

When they had sat down, Li Yuanjun asked, "Shall I pour you a cup of water? I will put the jug down between us in case you want a refill later."

"With pleasure," He Weimin replied and took the cup, which Li Yuanjun pushed into his outstretched hand. "The training was very helpful. I had almost forgotten what it's like to practice with others."

"I am also glad to finally have a worthy training partner again," Li Yuanjun said, pouring himself a cup of water. "Su Tao and Cai Long, with whom I used to train a lot, hardly have time for me anymore. They are always busy with each other and exclude me."

He realized how childish he sounded and hurried to add, "But their work as teacher and blacksmith keep them busy." To get back on track, he took a deep sip of water. "Hmm, what's that flavor?"

"I added some peppermint leaves to the water to keep it fresh for longer," He Weimin answered, turning his face away.

Did He Weimin do this for him? Li Yuanjun shook his head at this absurd thought. The water yesterday had probably contained another ingredient that he hadn't noticed: yarrow or those flowers with the small yellow blossoms.

"Don't you like it? I should have asked you if you like peppermint first," stammered He Weimin.

"It is very refreshing. You're really good with flowers and herbs."

"It is a part of my education," He Weimin dismissed the compliment. However, he couldn't stop a slight blush from creeping up his neck.

To take He Weimin's mind elsewhere, Li Yuanjun asked, "What kind of magnificent sword do you have?"

Li Yuanjun had already noticed during training that He Weimin's sword emitted a strong magical aura. He just hadn't found the right opportunity to ask him about it yet.

"Sword."

"What?" Li Yuanjun thought he had misheard.

Chapter 5
Two Swords

"The name of this sword is Sword," He Weimin explained with a tense smile on his face.

Now, Li Yuanjun understood what He Weimin had meant but considered his answer insufficient, so he immediately followed up. "Who came up with that unimaginative name?"

He Weimin had already opened his mouth to reply when Li Yuanjun added, giggling, "It's a very useful name. It's certainly easy to remember in a battle."

Li Yuanjun had only wanted to tease and amuse He Weimin, but his expression became increasingly gloomy.

"The name was chosen by my uncle Huiliang, from whom I inherited Sword. I didn't rename it to honor him." The final words left his mouth in a whisper. Li Yuanjun felt like slapping himself for his ignorance.

Li Yuanjun put his cup down next to the jug. He had already raised one hand to put it on He Weimin's arm in a comforting gesture. Just in time, he remembered how He Weimin had flinched at the gesture yesterday and lowered his hand.

"Weimin, I certainly didn't mean to disrespect your uncle. Please forgive me, and let me make up for it."

"There is nothing to make up for," He Weimin said after taking a sip of his water. "It wasn't your comment that hurt me, but the memories of my uncle."

"Then perhaps we should talk about something other than our weapons," Li Yuanjun suggested.

"Unnecessary. I just wasn't prepared for it. Feel free to ask what you want to know."

He Weimin touched the tassel of Sword which was the same color as his clothes. Li Yuanjun would have loved to hear the story about Sword, but wanted to give He Weimin a breather first.

"Guess what? I will tell you about my sword, then you can tell me what Sword is all about."

When he saw He Weimin nodding, he continued. "This is Gemini Bastard. Would you like to hold her?"

"Her?" He Weimin asked.

Now, Li Yuanjun had to laugh. "Yes, you heard me right. My sword is a she. You're the first to mention it. Everyone else wants to know what the bastard is all about."

"May I take a look at her?" He Weimin made sure and stretched out his palms.

Li Yuanjun took Bastard out of its sheath and carefully placed it in He Weimin's hands so as not to hurt him.

He Weimin began to carefully feel the sword's contours. Li Yuanjun looked at He Weimin's hands with their long, slender fingers. He used them to trace the patterns on Bastard's hilt. While watching this, Li Yuanjun felt a fluttering in his stomach. To distract himself, he turned his gaze to the ground, where the sun was forming a mosaic of shadows through the oak tree's leaves.

31

"Bastard's blade is red. I had a sheath made in the matching color," he explained.

"Red," He Weimin muttered to himself.

"Yes, I insisted on red," said Li Yuanjun. "Isn't it ironic that a sword called Bastard is the color of weddings?"

"Well, red also represents luck. I think it suits your personality," He Weimin replied.

Before Li Yuanjun could think more carefully about what He Weimin meant by this statement, he had finished his reflections yet kept Bastard in his hands.

"Why Gemini?" He Weimin wanted to know. "She doesn't have a double blade."

Most people always lingered on the term *Bastard*. Only when Li Yuanjun's tension eased did he realize that he had secretly hoped He Weimin would ignore this fact.

"Back then, I was young and lacked judgment and always had to stick my neck out, no matter who I hurt in the process," Li Yuanjun said calmly. "I disregarded my grandmother's warning and embarked on a quest that almost killed me."

"How old were you then?" He Weimin asked, handing Bastard back to Li Yuanjun.

"I had just turned fourteen and already thought I was a man. If I hadn't met Smaq and Kniq, the water god Ticulgubh's twin sons, my grandmother would have had to bury another family member. Assuming they have had found my corpse at all."

Li Yuanjun looked at the blades of grass, the tips of which were moved by a faint breeze. Deeply immersed in memories, he almost missed He Weimin's question.

"You mean your mother, Li Meifen. Li Xifeng told me about her. She was not only spirited but also a beauty."

"Indeed, that's what she tells everybody. I got her personality but, unfortunately, my father's looks. I wish I looked more like her, then I could remember her more easily when I look in the mirror," he said, lost in thoughts.

"Your father isn't . . ."

"He's a famous ruler who doesn't know he has a son. Or the head of a clan whose legitimate children were murdered by his enemies, which is why he's keeping me hidden. Maybe he died before I was even born."

Li Yuanjun's grip tightened around Bastard, which he was holding on his lap, and his voice became softer and softer. "I don't know anything about him. He didn't even see fit to bequeath me a telltale mole."

When Li Yuanjun turned to look at He Weimin, his expression reflected his own feelings. There was no sign of the rejection he had feared.

"As you can see, I am the Bastard who doesn't even know his father's name."

He Weimin reached out for Li Yuanjun with his hand and placed it on his knee. Li Yuanjun hadn't even realized that he had bent his legs and wrapped his arms around them.

"Your brother Su Tao . . ."

"He was adopted by my mother. His parents abandoned him at the Nia River when he was six years old. They had told him to follow the river until he came across a village. If he had walked toward the Shawree Mountains instead of the Yaosen, he would have died."

"Su Tao's parents probably aren't cultivators," He Weimin guessed.

"In any case, he wouldn't be the first child to be abandoned because of his powers," Li Yuanjun stated thoughtfully. "Although cultivators are respected by society, they also cause fear. Parents who do not cultivate are often overwhelmed by a child with powers."

"Human beings often fear what they don't understand," He Weimin agreed. "Su Tao was lucky to be accepted at the Yaosen and have you as a brother. Although you are not related by blood, you two get along well."

"The closest friends, even if he's always stuck with Cai Long lately."

"And the twin gods helped you obtain Bastard?" He Weimin steered the conversation in its original direction.

"I wouldn't necessarily call it 'help'. Let's just say they pointed out my stupidity because they were even dumber than me and had lost their way in the Shawree Mountains. Their father gave me Bastard out of gratitude for getting them back.

Smaq and Kniq naturally insisted on 'helping' me name my new weapon. They said that the name should remind me of our great adventure for the rest of my life. I still don't know if they even know what a bastard is. They must know the term from one of their adventure novels that they love so much."

He Weimin went to withdraw his hand, which Li Yuanjun prevented by placing his own on top of it. He himself did not know why this small gesture meant so much to him.

"Being on a quest at the age of fourteen and returning with a magical weapon is impressive. I can hardly compete with that since Sword was more or less given to me as a gift," He Weimin said appreciatively. "Do you still want to hear the story?"

"Of course, I love stories. Uhm . . . what I mean to say is that it's always an advantage to know your opponent's weapon as well as possible. Any information can be decisive in a battle," Li Yuanjun stated.

"Since when are we enemies?"

"Obviously, we are not enemies," Li Yuanjun relented. "We will be practicing against each other often. I think you're ready for a practice match. We should begin it tomorrow."

How would He Weimin react to this brazen request? To distract himself, Li Yuanjun wanted to take a sip of water but realized too late that his cup was already empty. As he was not yet ready to let go of

He Weimin's hand to get a refill, he quickly grabbed the jug to drink straight out of it.

"So, I guess I will have to tell you the whole story of my sword in order not to obtain an advantage over you," He Weimin said.

Li Yuanjun already thought he had offended He Weimin until the latter turned to him with a smile on his face.

"You could just admit that you like listening to stories."

"Everybody loves to hear a good story, and if it involves magic weapons, monsters, and virgins to be rescued, all the better."

"Who mentioned virgins?"

"They're always part of it. Otherwise, where's the incentive for the adventure?"

"I thought the adventure was incentive enough."

"I won't answer that and will remain silent in offense," Li Yuanjun said, nudging He Weimin lightly with his elbow.

Smiling, He Weimin raised the cup in Li Yuanjun's approximate direction with his free hand. "May I please have some more of that water, or has it already run out?"

It had not gone unnoticed by Li Yuanjun that He Weimin had made no attempt to free his hand. He shook the jug to show that there was still some water left inside. "You can have the rest, but you should know that I drank directly from the jug earlier." Li Yuanjun had remembered how He Weimin had wiped the jug after drinking yesterday.

"I appreciate your honesty. Since we already drank from the same jug yesterday, we should be able to do the same today, as we aren't strangers, after all."

Li Yuanjun filled He Weimin's cup and noticed that the sky had clouded again. "It's getting dark early today, and it might even rain. Shall we go back to Yaosen together? You could tell me the story about Sword on the way."

"You are right; the weather is changing. I can tell from the decrease in temperature that the sun is no longer shining, and the humidity is increasing. It wouldn't be wise to stay here any longer." He Weimin resolutely drank his cup in a few sips and put it away in his sleeve pocket.

Li Yuanjun handed He Weimin his own empty cup so that he could pack it up, too. He wanted to carry the jug himself. When He Weimin took his hand off Li Yuanjun's knee, he left a warm imprint that slowly cooled. He comforted himself with the thought that he could now enjoy He Weimin's company all the way to the Yaosen.

The two cultivators stood up, with Li Yuanjun knocking a few blades of grass off his coat. As He Weimin bent down to pick up his cloth, Li Yuanjun glanced furtively at the back of him to check for any grass stains. There were no stains and no blades of grass.

Quite a shame, he thought, but he immediately banished the thought before the mushrooms in his stomach could remind him again.

He Weimin, who hadn't noticed Li Yuanjun's inner turmoil, was ready to leave. Li Yuanjun hooked his forearm through He Weimin's, who had bent his arm as a precaution. A glance at the sky showed him that they still had plenty of time and didn't need to hurry.

While Li Yuanjun guided He Weimin across the glade, He Weimin seemed to be thinking about where to start telling his story. When he eventually began to tell it, Li Yuanjun almost tripped. He was grateful for the support of He Weimin's arm.

"Back in the day, it all started with the Quarrelsome Concubine."

Chapter 6

THE QUARRELSOME CONCUBINE

"Please don't tell me there was a fight over a woman," Li Yuanjun said.

"Not *a* concubine, but the Quarrelsome Concubine," corrected He Weimin. "That was the name of my uncle's first sword. Before he came into possession of Sword, he had managed to obtain a very powerful sword through a quest when he was nineteen years old."

"So that must have been the Concubine?" Li Yuanjun asked.

"Yes, correct," He Weimin confirmed, "except the fact she didn't have that name back then. My uncle wasn't able to find a suitable name for this magical weapon."

Li Yuanjun unsuccessfully tried to suppress a laugh. Right on time, he prevented He Weimin from getting caught on a sapling. The path was not made for two grown men walking side by side.

"You were lucky that he was your uncle and not your father. Imagine if he had numbered his children and given you a number instead of a name."

"He wasn't my father, but we grew up almost like brothers."

"Wasn't he older than you?" Li Yuanjun wondered.

"Just a couple of years," explained He Weimin. "He was the youngest of my mother's four brothers. I myself have three younger brothers and two sisters, making me the oldest of us children."

"Then perhaps I should call you *first son* from now on?" Li Yuanjun mocked.

"Don't you dare, and stop fooling around."

"I will not stop because the truth is you like it." Li Yuanjun had stopped to make sure that He Weimin's face was smiling.

"You're no better than your students. Their behavior is probably rubbing off on you."

"And you're not an old man yet. We're almost the same age."

"I am thirty-eight years old. That makes me an elder you should treat with respect."

"So, with respect, lower your head now so you don't bump it on the low-hanging branch on your left side."

He Weimin followed Li Yuanjun's advice. The confidence this gesture expressed sent a warm tingle through Li Yuanjun's chest.

"And after your uncle pondered over a name for his sword for a long time, he decided on the Quarrelsome Concubine," Li Yuanjun returned to the topic at hand, not wanting to dwell on his strange feelings.

"The Concubine chose her own name," explained He Weimin. "Because my uncle had waited so long to give her a name, she developed a mind of her own. She refused to obey him, and there was nothing he could do about it in his inexperience. When he called her 'no better than a quarrelsome concubine' during a drinking session, she took it as an act of naming."

Li Yuanjun gripped his sword with his free hand. "I must have been lucky once again that Bastard is so easy to care for," he noted.

He Weimin hung his head, probably remembering what was to follow.

"My uncle would have preferred to banish the Concubine to the armory and use his old sword from his training days again. But his father was against it, as it would have been a loss of honor for the family."

"Your uncle seems to have been a pragmatic person. What happened?"

"I was fifteen or sixteen years old at the time and didn't yet own my magical weapon. Nevertheless, my uncle constantly encouraged me to accompany him on his travels. My parents didn't mind. 'After all, a teenager has to gain experience in battle,' they always said. They couldn't accompany me themselves because they had to look after my younger siblings, who were still toddlers at the time."

Li Yuanjun shook his head. "I'm impressed that you'd already taken part in serious battles at this age. For us at the Yaosen, a quest is often the first test in battle."

"Which you completed at the age of fourteen."

"Well, yes. But the sensible ones wait until at least after their twentieth birthday."

"But I didn't even earn a sword during a quest," He Weimin objected.

"Earning a magical artifact on a quest is honorable, but making a foreign weapon submit to your will is no easy task, as we have witnessed with your uncle," Li Yuanjun said.

"It happened during a night hunt that I accompanied my uncle on. Under favorable conditions, my uncle was able to lead the Quarrelsome Concubine according to his will. That night, however, there were other clans and schools involved in the hunt. Since a large bounty had been placed on the prey, competition quickly developed among the cultivators."

Li Yuanjun kicked an interfering branch out of the way with his foot. "Some people still want more. They don't care who they harm in the process."

"My uncle lost his right hand that night, which he had used to guide the Quarrelsome Concubine. The bleeding was stopped, and my uncle's life was saved, but he was no longer able to fight with a sword afterward. The Concubine also refused to release the severed hand and remained magically bound to it. She didn't want anyone to give her orders ever again."

Their steps had slowed down imperceptibly during He Weimin's description until they had come to a complete stop. Li Yuanjun realized from He Weimin's tense posture that he had not yet finished his story. He placed the jug on the ground next to him and put his hand on He Weimin's, which felt cold.

The gesture seemed to calm He Weimin down a little so that he was able to continue speaking. "Due to the high blood loss and shock, my uncle suffered from a severe fever for weeks. My family had little hope that my uncle would recover. I spent a lot of time with him back then and told him about all the things we would experience when he finally got better.

Contrary to expectations, his health did improve. Without the burden of the Concubine, he regained his will to live."

Li Yuanjun thought that was the end of the story until He Weimin continued speaking.

"As soon as my uncle was able to get up, he went to our clan's training ground. He grabbed one of the training swords with his left hand and began to practice. In the weeks, months, and years that followed, I was his only training partner."

He Weimin's face, which had previously lost its color, became more and more red. "You can stop rubbing my hand. It's still there."

Not even noticing that he had started stroking He Weimin's hand, Li Yuanjun winced. At least it was warm again now. He stopped moving but left his hand where it was.

"It took almost three years for my uncle to become as skillful at fighting with his left arm as he had been with his right. Eventually, his efforts paid off, and during his second quest, he once again managed to acquire a magical sword. Even before he returned to our clan, he named his new weapon Sword."

Li Yuanjun turned to He Weimin, who looked as if he wanted to say something else. When he remained silent, Li Yuanjun interjected, "Truly an interesting story. Now that you're the owner of Sword, it doesn't seem to be over yet."

"We will arrive at the Yaosen in a few meters; perhaps we should save the rest of the story for tomorrow after training." Li Yuanjun reluctantly let go of He Weimin's hand to reach for the jug.

Right when he uttered these words, Li Yuanjun realized that it was more than just an excuse to spend time with He Weimin. He wanted to learn as much as possible about him. After all, He Weimin intended to return to his family soon.

"You have a penchant for stories," He Weimin stated matter-of-factly.

"I don't. No more than anyone else, anyway. So, what do you say? Is it a deal? After all, we're already sworn brothers because of the secret of the glade."

"You sound like a character from one of your adventure novels."

When they stepped out of the forest, Li Yuanjun was dazzled by the light of the magic lamps.

"The path is very familiar to me now. I can easily walk it alone," He Weimin said, intending to release Li Yuanjun's arm and trying to hide his expression.

This was the He Weimin that Li Yuanjun had known before. However, he would no longer allow him to keep his distance as easily as before.

"As you prefer, but I will still accompany you to your apartment. It is on my way home, anyway. We can also get something to eat at the Blue Pearl, or would you like to eat there right away?"

"I would prefer to eat in my apartment if you don't mind."

"That's fine with me; then we'll take the food with us."

Li Yuanjun knew that He Weimin usually ate in his room. He had always assumed that He Weimin found it too difficult to walk to the restaurant. He imagined that he would have to cross the Nia River, which wound its way through the Yaosen compound, in complete darkness. The very thought sent a chill up the back of his neck.

When they arrived at the Blue Pearl, it turned out they were the only guests. Most of the Yaosen residents had already eaten dinner and returned to their homes. The interior of the building was pleasantly cool and, in keeping with the mushroom season, exuded the smell of mushroom dishes.

The dining room consisted of around ten tables, which could be moved together as required. There was also a wooden counter where patrons could eat.

They got the last portions of the dish of the day, which turned out to be rice with mushrooms, wrapped up.

Li Yuanjun juggled the two food containers and the water jug as he went to open the door of the Blue Pearl. Lai Meixiu, the daughter of the owners of the Blue Pearl, who had served them and then started to clean the taproom, reached past him to help as he walked past.

"Come on out, gentlemen," she said with a smile on her face.

"Thank you, Meixiu," Li Yuanjun said. "My greetings to your mum. Your food is delicious as always, even though I can hardly wait for the mushroom season to be over. Without meat on my plate, I'm still wasting away."

"The door is a meter in front of you. Watch the threshold." He turned to He Weimin, who was walking behind him.

When Lai Meixiu had closed the door behind them, the cool evening air greeted them. The sky was dotted with stars after it had cleared. The same could not be said for He Weimin, whose brow furrowed and lips formed a line.

"What's going on with you all of a sudden?"

"It's nothing, let's go," He Weimin replied in a calm voice, too calm.

"It's most certainly not 'nothing'. Is it because of Lai Meixiu? Are you jealous?" Li Yuanjun couldn't keep himself from asking.

Chapter 7

Curfew

He Weimin's expression became calm, and he moved a hand over his head. "Of course, I'm not jealous. You could be Lai Meixiu's father, and you're just being nice to her. Furthermore, I have no interest in young ladies." He had paused before speaking the last words.

"So, what is it about?" Li Yuanjun wanted to know. "Tell me. Otherwise, I will hold your dinner hostage."

He Weimin hesitated and rubbed his palms against his thighs. "I am useless. I can't help you carry or hold the door for you, which even a child could," he burst out.

"Come on, let's walk for a while," Li Yuanjun said. "Just because you can't do some things doesn't mean you're useless. My grandmother is over three hundred years old and can't even boil an egg. Our alchemist, Deng Tingfeng, wouldn't even be able to give a compliment if his life depended on it. And I couldn't be made to stop talking without a silencing spell. Perhaps not even with a spell like that . . ."

"I'm certain of the latter, but not so much about the other two things."

"There you go, it's fine," Li Yuanjun said with satisfaction. "That's exactly the smile I want to see on your face. Now take the jug and give me your forearm so we can get there today."

In a familiar manner, Li Yuanjun led He Weimin along the path across the bridge over the River Nia to the house that He Weimin shared with two of the older students.

Li Yuanjun could already see the light shining through the windows of the house from afar. He Weimin's roommates were already at home. Disappointment spread through him. He had hoped to have dinner alone with He Weimin. He shook his head at himself. Where would his roommates be at this time of night if not at home?

When they arrived at the one-story building, they stopped in front of the door. Li Yuanjun reluctantly let go of He Weimin's arm and didn't know what to do with his now free hand.

"Here we are," he said, just to break the silence. He felt like a schoolboy who had accompanied his first date home, only not to know what to do.

That decision was taken from him by an opening door that almost threw him to the floor.

"There's Weimin. And in one piece, too." They were greeted by a giant with a serious face and hair sticking out in all directions. "And Yuanjun." He was greeted with a nod.

"I told you we don't have to worry about him. He can take care of himself, and if he does get lost, he will certainly be able to send out a magical signal," a second voice intervened.

On closer inspection, Li Yuanjun noticed that the voice belonged to Xue Mengyao, who was trying to squeeze past Dai Liuxian, who was almost blocking the entire doorway. With his long, light blonde hair and petite stature, Xue Mengyao could almost be mistaken for a girl. As soon as he opened his mouth, however, this assumption was quickly forgotten.

"We were just going to look for Weimin, but the Meng'er couldn't find his trousers. Luckily, you brought him back safely." Dai Liuxian turned to Li Yuanjun.

The man in question glanced to see that the trousers had reappeared and were safely attached to Xue Mengyao's lower body.

"I didn't know you had a curfew." Li Yuanjun turned to He Weimin, unable to keep a laugh out of his voice.

He Weimin's face turned bright red right up to the tips of his ears. "Me neither. They just think they have to look after me all the time." Turning to his roommates, he added, "I told you I was going to train after work. You don't have to wait for me. And now leave us alone so we can say goodbye."

When the door had closed behind them, Li Yuanjun whispered, "You think they're eavesdropping behind the door?"

He Weimin shook his head but then shrugged his shoulders. "No, or yes, maybe. Let's take a few steps to the side, just in case. They're really nice and helpful people, but sometimes they behave like overprotective parents toward me, even though they're ten years younger than me." He Weimin couldn't suppress a shudder, which made Li Yuanjun laugh.

"I suppose your roommates go to bed early as they've already been to bed?" he wanted to know.

"They do," said He Weimin with a petrified face.

"Well, in that case, let's say goodbye soon-ish before they think you've gone missing. Stretch out your arm so I can give you your food."

He Weimin took the container with his portion. This particular movement drew Li Yuanjun's gaze to the jug He Weimin was still holding in his other hand.

"Guess what? Tomorrow I'm going to provide the drinks. You can bring the cups." With these words, Li Yuanjun took the jug out of He Weimin's hand, which the latter accepted without objection.

"So we'll meet tomorrow for a practice match at the glade," said He Weimin.

"Oh yes, our practice match. I had forgotten all about that. We haven't even decided on a prize for the winner yet."

"Does there have to be a prize?" He Weimin wanted to know.

"Of course, that's what makes it really interesting. Well, let's see, what would be a suitable prize?" Li Yuanjun looked around, hoping for some inspiration.

"We could take a trip to one of the villages nearby on your next day off, and the loser pays."

He Weimin shifted from one foot to the other. "I am not that comfortable around strangers and unfamiliar territory yet. Or maybe an invitation to dinner at the Blue Pearl," he made another suggestion.

As if on cue, they both started laughing. The meal in the Yaosen restaurant was free for the students as well as members. Therefore, the winner of tomorrow's fight would have no real sacrifice to make.

Li Yuanjun rubbed tears from his eyes, and his gaze landed on He Weimin.

"I have the perfect solution. The winner will receive a Kiss as a reward."

Chapter 8

A 'Sweet Kiss'

He Weimin stilled as if Li Yuanjun was suddenly speaking a foreign language. His eyes widened, and his face lost all color before the blood rushed back like a flash flood. The food container swayed dangerously in his hand, trying to hold on to something with the other.

Li Yuanjun didn't know what had caused the reaction. With his hands fully packed, he was only able to walk toward He Weimin to offer him something to lean on should it become necessary.

"Do you need help? Is there anything I can do for you?" asked Li Yuanjun.

He Weimin's stance had stabilized. He straightened up and brushed a non-existent strand of hair from his forehead. "Agreed. The winner gets a kiss from the loser."

Li Yuanjun didn't know whether He Weimin was just trying to distract from his weakness by agreeing. After all, it had been a long day, and He Weimin had to slowly get used to training again. He decided to ignore He Weimin's strange behavior for now.

"The way you describe it doesn't sound too appealing. I think the winner and the loser should share a Sweet Kiss with each other. That sounds like more fun, don't you think?"

"Whatever you say," He Weimin agreed, slowly making his way toward the front door. "Until tomorrow, then," he added.

"Until tomorrow afternoon, at the glade," Li Yuanjun repeated.

Li Yuanjun moved toward the house, wanting to make sure that He Weimin got there safely. However, he had already been met by his roommates, who must have been watching their conversation through the glass window of the door.

"Bye, Yuanjun," Xue Mengyao bid him farewell.

"See you around. Thank you for bringing the Weimin back safely," Dai Liuxian said in his foreign dialect, closing the door behind them.

Li Yuanjun paused in the light streaming through the window on the door while wondering what had just happened. He really felt like the teenager who had just delivered his date safely to the parents.

To dispel this disturbing thought, Li Yuanjun shook his head. He was about to go home when he noticed the empty jug in his hand. To take his mind off it, he decided to buy the victory prize for tomorrow immediately.

Sweet Kiss was by far Li Yuanjun's favorite wine. The Yaosen often referred to it simply as Kiss, though. Although a meal invitation was out of the question as a prize for the practice match, Li Yuanjun could invite He Weimin for a drink.

So Li Yuanjun headed toward the Blue Pearl again, hoping that it was still open and that someone would sell him the wine.

As soon as he arrived at the inn, he was relieved to see that the lights were still on. He knocked on the door, which was already locked from the inside.

Lai Meixiu opened the door for him. "It's you," she said in surprise. "Have you forgotten something, or would you like to visit me?"

In Li Yuanjun's mind, Lai Meixiu was still the little girl with long pigtails and scraped knees. He was surprised to realize that she had grown up without him noticing. She had to be eighteen or nineteen by now.

"I'd like to buy a jug of your Sweet Kiss if it's not too late."

"Oh, and I was hoping you wanted to see me," Lai Meixiu said and winked at him. "I will forgive you this once, though. Come on in." She took a step back to let him in.

Li Yuanjun entered the Blue Pearl, and Lai Meixiu closed the door behind him. "How many times have I told you that you're too young for me?" he asked with mock seriousness.

"Like a trillion times, more or less. I'm just kidding," she responded to his joking tone. "Now give me your jug so I can fill it up."

He handed the jug to Lai Meixiu and followed her to the bar counter to watch her work.

Lai Meixiu turned to look at Li Yuanjun. "Besides, I stay away from taken men. It only creates problems."

"You're already talking like a widow in her prime. When did you learn . . . Wait, what did you say? I'm not taken."

"I might still be young, but during my work at the Blue Pearl, I learned to read the faces of the guests. When you look at He Weimin, you make this face." Lai Meixiu leaned forward, widened her eyes, opened her mouth, and dropped her jaw.

"Nonsense, you made that up. Besides, nobody makes a face like that."

"If you say so," Lai Meixiu said, handing him the filled jug across the counter.

"By the way, how's the baby? I haven't spotted a new wine name on the menu yet," he said, frantically trying to change the subject.

"Little Enlai is a real sweetheart. He sleeps all day, and at night, he keeps us all awake with his cries. My parents haven't even got round to thinking of a name for the new wine due to lack of sleep."

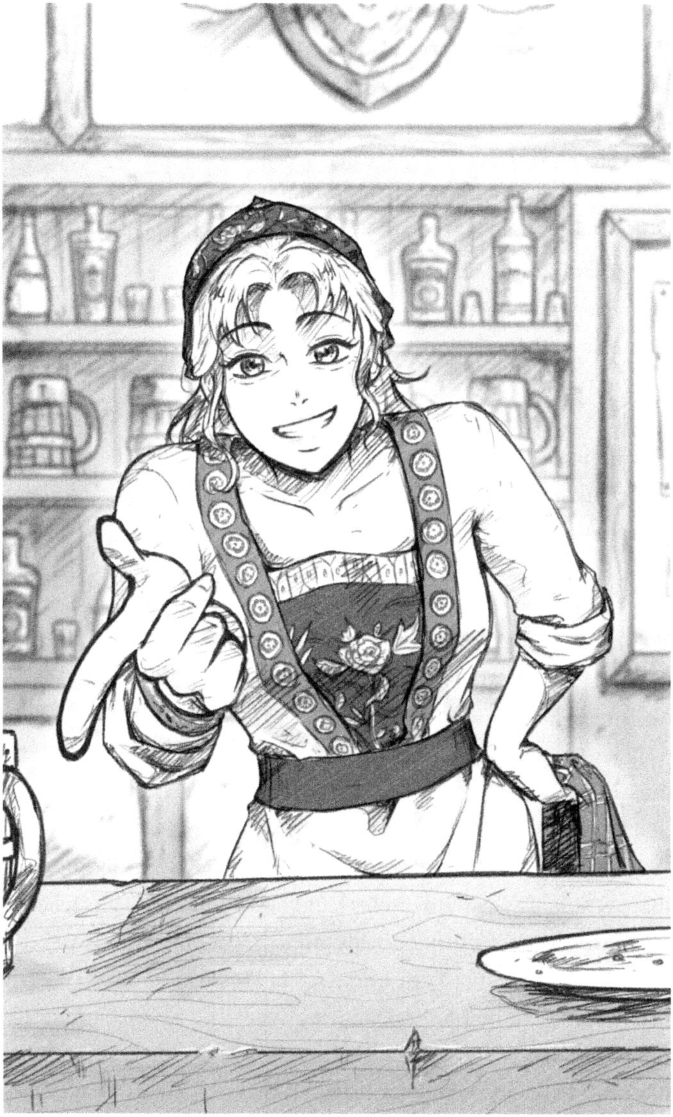

The Blue Pearl was famous for its wines, which were also exported. It was common knowledge at the Yaosen that the couple who ran the pub named their best creations after the birth of their children.

"Just like a normal baby," Li Yuanjun noted. "You could call the wine Sleepless at the Yaosen or The Scream."

"I don't know why my parents wanted an eighth child. The house is already crowded with them," Lai Meixiu complained with a smile on her face that belied her words.

"Who did your parents name first, you or Sweet Kiss?" Li Yuanjun wanted to know.

"For today, we're closed," said Lai Meixiu, throwing the cloth she had used to polish the counter at Li Yuanjun, ignoring his question. "I will put the wine on your tab; enjoy you two!"

Li Yuanjun dodged the bullet with ease. "How do you know I want to drink the wine with Weimin?"

"You just told me yourself," Lai Meixiu joked and put on the face. "Cheeky brat, that . . ."

He was interrupted by the roar of a baby, which made them both flinch. "Close the door behind you," Lai Meixiu said and sank down on one of the chairs next to the bar.

"Have a good night's sleep, too," Li Yuanjun, like the adult he was, couldn't help but say to Lai Meixiu when he was almost out the door.

When the Blue Pearl's door closed behind him for the second time that evening, Li Yuanjun ran his hand over his face. He was relieved to feel that he wasn't making a silly grimace. Lai Meixiu had just been teasing him. He couldn't be interested in He Weimin this way. That would ruin their budding friendship.

He inhaled deeply through his nose and exhaled through his mouth. He could only hope that Lai Meixiu wouldn't make that kind of comment when He Weimin was around. He would run for the hills at such an idea.

Li Yuanjun walked the short distance to his house, stopping every now and then to check that his face had not turned into a grimace.

Back home, he ate his mushroom soup, which had gone cold, and tried not to stare at the jug of wine all the time. He finally gave up his efforts and hid the jug next to the dirty dishes from dinner, which he also didn't want to see again until the next morning.

Before going to bed, he meditated. That was something he had neglected a lot recently. However, it did not bring him the rest he longed for at night, and he was haunted by confused dreams that he could no longer remember in the morning.

THE NEXT DAY, THE summer sun rose to power. There was not a single cloud in the sky, and the birds were loudly greeting the new day. Li Yuanjun, who had overslept, walked briskly to the training ground.

While he did, he tied his waist-length hair up with a ribbon. The braid turned out slightly askew as he was carrying the jug of wine in one hand.

Several eager students were already waiting for him on the training ground. When they saw the jug, they looked at him questioningly but did not dare to speak to him about it. Li Yuanjun put the jug away together with Bastard and took one of the blunt training swords.

After almost being hit in the face by a female student with the sword, he managed not to think about Lai Meixiu's remarks for the rest of the day. He was so engrossed in his work that he hadn't even paid attention to whether He Weimin was already on his way to the glade that afternoon.

After Li Yuanjun had finished his lesson and completed his inspection walk, he grabbed Bastard and the jug. He straightened up and set off toward the forest. Li Yuanjun had to laugh at himself. He felt like a student setting off on his first quest.

On the path to the glade, he kicked the branches lying on the ground out of the way and whistled the melody of a song. He wanted Weimin to hear that he was on his way to him.

When he arrived at the edge of the glade, Li Yuanjun hesitated to enter after all. To break this habit, he reached into the branches blocking his path and pushed them apart.

"It's me, Yuanjun."

He Weimin had completed some exercises to warm up. When he heard Li Yuanjun, he turned in his direction.

"Hopefully, you don't mind that I have already started without you," he greeted Li Yuanjun.

Li Yuanjun walked toward He Weimin. "Of course not. I already had a chance to warm up while working with my students," he said. He had remembered just in time that He Weimin could not see his shaking head.

"Shall we train together first or start the practice match right away?" Li Yuanjun asked when he stood at He Weimin's place.

He Weimin hesitated to answer. "Maybe we should do some pair exercises to get a better idea of each other."

"Suit yourself; then let's not waste time. I am just going to get the jug and my coat to the oak quickly. It's pretty warm again today."

When Li Yuanjun returned, He Weimin had already taken up his fighting stance and pinned up his hair with a valuable-looking clip.

They spent some time practicing and comparing their skills with each other.

"We are about the same skill level, but our fighting styles are quite different," Li Yuanjun stated during a short pause.

"Well," He Weimin simply replied.

"In a real fight, we would complement each other very well, don't you think?" Li Yuanjun tried to get He Weimin to talk.

He Weimin bit his lip and nodded.

"The sun will set soon. There's just enough time for our practice match."

"In case it is already too late today, we can postpone it until tomorrow," He Weimin suggested, averting his eyes.

"It's not too dark yet, and we don't know what the weather will be like tomorrow. Besides, I don't want to miss out on my reward . . . I mean *our* reward, of course. Do you need a longer break?" Li Yuanjun tried to get to the bottom of He Weimin's strange behavior.

He Weimin tightened his shoulders as if he had made a momentous decision. "I am ready," he said with an expression that suggested the contrary.

Was He Weimin worried about the victory prize? Well, fortunately, Li Yuanjun had made provisions for that. He didn't care who won the match. What mattered to him instead was the time he was able to spend with He Weimin afterward.

Chapter 9

A Practice Match

The battle turned out just as Li Yuanjun had hoped. After some initial hesitation, He Weimin steadily gained confidence, which was also reflected in his fighting behavior. Li Yuanjun had to admit that He Weimin was already very good at compensating for the sense he had lost due to his blindness.

He Weimin moved across the forest ground with an ease that Li Yuanjun would never achieve with his more muscular shape. His strength lay in his power. He Weimin's was in his speed.

Despite the differences in fighting style, neither of them managed to gain a noticeable advantage. It became obvious to Li Yuanjun that the fight would not be decided by the opponents' skill but by their stamina.

Li Yuanjun was breathing increasingly heavily, while He Weimin had not even broken a sweat yet. He would soon no longer be able to fend off He Weimin's attacks. If Li Yuanjun did not want to forego victory, he had to act now. He still had enough stamina for one last lunge. This had to work so well that it would leave He Weimin no way out.

He Weimin's pace was unchanged, but he had started to conserve his own left side. Li Yuanjun had already noticed during their training that He Weimin favored attacks from the right or the front.

Li Yuanjun faked an attack from the right. He Weimin tried to fend off this maneuver, which Li Yuanjun took advantage of and aimed at his left side.

When he saw He Weimin's unprotected left side, he unconsciously held his breath. Only after Bastard's broadside touched He Weimin's hip did he expel the air again.

He Weimin paused in his movement and fumbled for Li Yuanjun's weapon. The blow could have caused life-threatening injuries in a real fight. At the very least, the opponent would have been incapacitated.

To signal that the fight was over, He Weimin sheathed Sword. "Congratulations, you have truly earned your victory." With a bow, He Weimin acknowledged Li Yuanjun's victory.

Li Yuanjun stowed Bastard in the scabbard at his waist. "You fought well, too. I will have to try harder next time if I want to stand a chance."

"I accept the challenge. You were right to insist on training together. I've only just realized how much I have missed the practice battles with my peers," said He Weimin.

He Weimin's words didn't quite match his expressions. During the battle, unlike Li Yuanjun, he seemed rested and fresh. Now, he was swaying slightly, and his face was getting paler.

"I think we deserve a break now," Li Yuanjun said. Perhaps He Weimin just needed some rest to recover from the fight.

When He Weimin just pressed his lips tightly together and nodded, Li Yuanjun continued, "Why don't we have a seat under our oak tree in the shade?"

He Weimin turned to Li Yuanjun and inhaled deeply through his nose. "Alright then, let's take a short break before it's time to return."

That sounds more like He Weimin, Li Yuanjun thought, but it wasn't enough to bring the color back to his face.

Before Li Yuanjun could say anything back, He Weimin had already turned toward the oak tree and was about to leave.

"Wait for me." Li Yuanjun tried to make him stop. "Give me your arm, it will be faster." At least he would be able to support He Weimin this way, if necessary.

After a moment of hesitation, He Weimin bent his arm. Li Yuanjun took this as consent and grabbed the proffered arm. They slowly walked toward the oak tree, with He Weimin taking deep breaths. Li Yuanjun tried to warm up He Weimin's cold hand by rubbing it with his free hand.

When they reached the trees, Li Yuanjun helped He Weimin to sit down. He was so lost in thought that he accepted the action without objection.

Li Yuanjun remembered too late to provide He Weimin with a cloth. He reassured himself with the thought that he would be there to check He Weimin's clothes for dirt. He decided to give He Weimin some rest and let his eyes wander over him in the meantime.

For someone who had undergone several hours of training, He Weimin looked surprisingly organized, except for his pale face. Although this day was very hot, He Weimin had refrained from taking off his coat. A single strand of hair had come loose from his elaborate hairstyle. Li Yuanjun just managed to stop himself from tucking it behind He Weimin's ear to restore his immaculate appearance.

Li Yuanjun stroked his own red hair, which was only loosely held together by the ribbon.

Although he liked the peaceful silence, He Weimin's fingers tightening around the grass and its lingering paleness made him want to break it. "How can you stand it in your clothes in this heat without suffocating?"

"Because of the breathing. It's a special breathing technique that slows down the heartbeat," He Weimin gasped.

"It doesn't seem to be working out too well at the moment." Li Yuanjun couldn't hold back a comment.

"No," He Weimin managed to get out and made a strange motion with his hand.

"Are you feeling hot?" Li Yuanjun tried to interpret the gesture. "Listen, I took off my coat before training and untied my shirt. Maybe you should take off your coat, too, so you can breathe better?"

Was this a shaking head or a nod that He Weimin was trying to make? "No worries, I won't tell anyone either. Your reputation is in good hands with me." Without waiting for an answer, Li Yuanjun grabbed He Weimin's coat to help him out.

As Li Yuanjun fiddled with He Weimin's coat, He Weimin's condition seemed to deteriorate further. He now looked as if he would start spitting up blood at any moment.

Li Yuanjun paused in his endeavors. "You cannot breathe. Should I call for help?"

Without warning, He Weimin reached for Li Yuanjun and groped over his upper body with trembling hands until he grabbed him by the collar. Li Yuanjun froze. He was now at eye level with He Weimin and waited with bated breath to see what He Weimin would do.

He Weimin was breathing more heavily now, so at least he seemed to be getting his breath back. Li Yuanjun closed his eyes and hoped that he would not be hit by a gush of blood from He Weimin's mouth. What happened next was something Li Yuanjun would never have dreamed of.

Chapter 10

The Winner's Reward

The first kiss hit Li Yuanjuns nose. The second landed on the forehead. The third was a straight hit.

He could not have been more surprised if He Weimin had a *Qi* deviation right in front of him. He opened his eyes and blinked several times to convince himself that he hadn't just imagined these kisses.

But no, there was no doubt about it; it was He Weimin's lips gently touching his mouth. *How strange it is that He Weimin has his eyes closed even though he can't see anything*, the weird thought crossing his mind.

He Weimin was now exerting a little more pressure without Li Yuanjun being able to move. It was only when He Weimin's unmistakable soapy scent caught his nose that he was shaken out of his stupor. Before he could return the kiss, He Weimin let go of his collar and leaned back.

"Was this enough?"

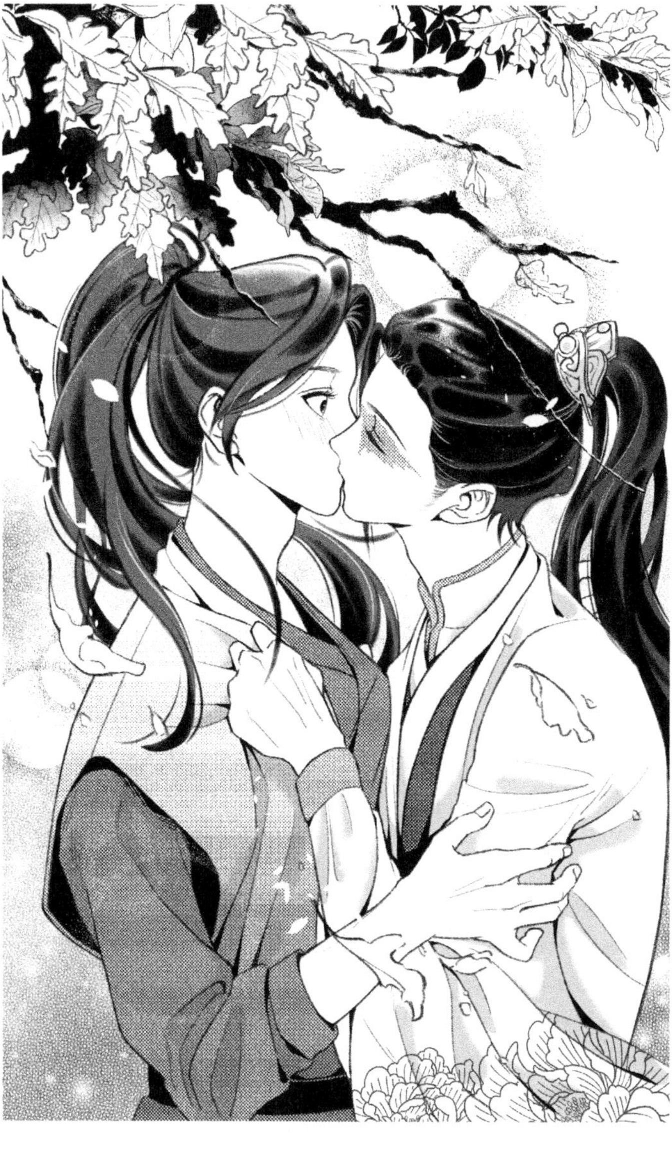

Li Yuanjun's head was spinning, and he only now noticed that he had raised his arms as if to reach for He Weimin. What was He Weimin talking about? They had only just started. How could that be enough?

When Li Yuanjun remained silent, He Weimin explained, "The reward for the winner of the practice match. Is my debt paid?"

Li Yuanjun's foggy mind needed some time to capture what He Weimin was getting at. Did He Weimin misunderstand him and thought that Sweet Kiss meant a real kiss and not the wine of that name? *That can't be true*, Li Yuanjun figured, a burning sensation spreading through his stomach.

He opened his mouth, which seemed to be parched, but no words came out. He Weimin must have heard about the Sweet Kiss over the past year. Li Yuanjun had seen him drink the wine himself. Such a mix-up was simply not possible.

At any moment, He Weimin would burst out laughing and be amused at how he had tricked Li Yuanjun. He Weimin's expression remained serious as he slowly stood up. "I am sorry," he said in an increasingly quiet voice.

Li Yuanjun wanted to grab He Weimin's coat to stop him. But He Weimin had already turned round and was moving away from him with more skill than Li Yuanjun would have given him credit for.

"Hold on," Li Yuanjun was still able to say without He Weimin responding. He didn't know whether He Weimin had stopped hearing him or was deliberately ignoring him. His body was frozen and didn't want to move. Motionless, he watched He Weimin move further and further away from him with stiff but sure steps.

His first impulse was to follow He Weimin to clear up the misunderstanding. He had already half risen when he let himself sink back into the grass with the flimsy explanation that He Weimin needed rest and time to think.

With a sigh, he stretched out on the ground and put his arm over his eyes. He was unable to banish He Weimin's receding figure from his thoughts. A few blades of grass had become entangled in He Weimins coat, and Li Yuanjun thought that he should have pointed this out to his friend.

Were they still friends at all? Perhaps Li Yuanjun had only convinced himself that He Weimin had also enjoyed their time together. He certainly hadn't expected the kiss, though.

The kiss. How must He Weimin have felt to feel compelled to kiss Li Yuanjun? He must have been so repulsed by the thought of it that he must have felt sick. Now, He Weimin's strange change in mood and his paleness after the fight made sense.

What did He Weimin think of him now? Li Yuanjun would never have suggested a real kiss as a wager, not even jokingly. Why had He Weimin agreed to the demand in the first place? Had he thought he had no choice?

Li Yuanjun let his arm slide away from his eyes and touched his mouth with his fingertips. Everything had happened so quickly earlier that he hadn't even noticed that He Weimin's lips, unlike his hands, weren't cold. Instead, they had felt pleasantly warm and soft.

Stop thinking about the kiss now, Li Yuanjun reminded himself. With a jerk, he straightened up and made sure that there was no sign of He Weimin. He should now have a big enough head start to be able to retreat.

Li Yuanjun stood up and walked where he had left his coat. Once there, his eyes fell on the jug of wine. He considered flushing down his feelings with the wine—the *Sweet Kiss*, as the voice in his mind reminded him.

He straightened and took his coat and the untouched wine. Waking up hungover tomorrow wouldn't help him fix the situation with He Weimin. He needed a clear head for that.

Slowly, deep in thought, he left the clearing. Being the coward that he was, he deliberately dawdled on his way home to avoid running into He Weimin after all.

The birds were surprisingly quiet, and the humidity had increased. Li Yuanjun hoped that it wouldn't rain tomorrow. He shook his head at himself. He Weimin was unlikely to come to the clearing tomorrow after today's events.

Lai Meixiu's words came back to his mind. Was it possible that he felt more for He Weimin than mere friendship? He had had many relationships in his thirty-five years of life, good and not-so-good, but there had been no love on his part.

Li Yuanjun's love life had become calm in recent years. The fleeting adventures of his youth had increasingly lost their appeal for him. He longed for a steady relationship and a partner with whom he had more in common than sexual attraction.

Li Yuanjun stepped on a twig lying on the path. He could hardly believe that it had only been the day before yesterday that he had been playing hide-and-seek with He Weimin here.

He thought back to the day when He Weimin had come to the Yaosen. It had also been late summer then, and he had gone to see his grandmother to tell her how sorry he was about his non-existent love life. She had only looked at him with one of her mysterious smiles and assured him that he would realize when he met true love.

Li Yuanjun stamped his foot and kicked two annoying branches out of the way. As if it was that easy.

He had laughed out loud at his grandmother's statement back then. Who would believe that the love of his life would simply walk through the door and strike him down? Before he could get a chance to ask Li Xifeng for more details, their conversation had been interrupted by the arrival of guests.

After Li Xifeng's conversation with He Weimin and his family had ended, she explained to Li Yuanjun that it was only a matter of time before he would find his answer. Until then, he could take care of their new arrival at Yaosen so that He Weimin could settle in more easily.

Taking care of him worked like a charm, Li Yuanjun scolded himself with self-mockery.

An idea appeared in Li Yuanjun's mind, and he almost tripped over his own feet. *No, it simply couldn't be.*

Li Yuanjun had only wanted to support the mysterious He Weimin back then. He had been attracted to him from the very beginning, and this interest had not vanished. In order to be able to spend more time with He Weimin, he had even insisted on bringing him his meals every day. A task that his overprotective roommates would certainly have been happy to do.

Even when He Weimin's behavior toward him had become increasingly dismissive, he had been unable to stay away from him. Had He Weimin noticed something about his feelings and tried to distance himself from him? Li Yuanjun's uneasiness in his stomach returned with a bang, and he broke out in a sweat. He had a feeling that perhaps this condition hadn't been caused by the mushrooms after all.

He felt his chest with one hand. Was his heart on the right, left, or in the center? If he had paid more attention in class when the acupressure points had been explained to them, he would know. Anyway, it still seemed to be there, even if it was beating a little too fast.

He set off again to cover the last few meters of the path to the Yaosen. That was just the way it was, and he had a little crush on He Weimin. So what? There is nothing wrong with it. After all, He Weimin didn't need to know about it.

Wait, did that mean he had already partially fallen in love with He Weimin? Was it even possible to fall in love just a little bit? Wasn't that already L...

The voice of reason, which he usually ignored, told him that he wouldn't get anywhere on his own and that he should seek professional help. So, when he stepped out of the shadows of the forest, he decided to turn to his friends Su Tao and Cai Long for advice.

Chapter 11

Friends

During this time of day, Cai Long and Su Tao were supposed to be at the smithy run by Cai Long. So Li Yuanjun headed straight in that direction.

The building that housed the smithy was two stories high, with a covered porch that allowed Cai Long to shoe the horses' hooves underneath. The entire lower floor was taken up by the workshop, which customers entered via an entrance under the porch. The upper floor served as Cai Long's apartment.

There was a second entrance at the back of the building, though. A corridor led to the workshop and a staircase to the upper floor. As the front door was already locked, Li Yuanjun used the back entrance.

As he stepped through the door, he was hit by a blast of hot air and the smell of leather. He closed the door behind him and stood still to acclimate to the heat. Voices from the direction of the workshop told him that his friends must have been there.

Li Yuanjun slowly walked to the workshop, the temperature still seeming to rise. As he had hoped, he found Cai Long and Su Tao there. The two turned their backs on him and were engrossed in conversation. They hadn't noticed him yet. The giant Cai Long had his arm around Su Tao. They were fiddling with an object lying on the worktop in front of them.

"What are you guys up to once again?" he greeted his friends.

The two flinched and moved apart, startled. When they turned to him at the same time, Su Tao hid the object behind his back.

"Nothing. Why would you think that?" Su Tao tried to distract them.

"We are working on, uhm . . . on a new weapon," Cai Long added, earning a kick to his ankle from Su Tao.

Li Yuanjun took a step forward and tried to catch a glimpse of the object, which Su Tao prevented with a skillful move.

"The last time you did *nothing*, it destroyed half the smithy," Li Yuanjun said with a meaningful look at the still soot-blackened walls.

"Using my dragon fire to raise the temperature of the forge fire was still a good idea," Cai Long defended the incident and looked up at the ceiling. "We just shouldn't have used it so close to the building," he added with slumped shoulders. For a muscular half-dragon over two meters tall, this gesture looked highly guilty.

"Be glad we didn't let you in on it. It saved you a scolding from our grandmother." Su Tao turned to Li Yuanjun, having managed to make the mysterious object disappear into a drawer.

"So, I was lucky once again. But I would have liked to see the big bang up close," Li Yuanjun could not stop himself from saying. He cast another appraising glance over Su Tao and Cai Long, who were still standing there like two children who had been caught doing something forbidden. Li Yuanjun had to suppress a laugh. He would find out what his friends were trying to hide from him this time.

A twinge in his stomach reminded Li Yuanjun of the reason for his visit. He rubbed his palms against his thighs and alternately looked Su Tao and Cai Long in the face.

"We gotta talk," he said in a low voice. Li Yuanjun straightened up and tried again: "I have something serious to discuss with you. Do you have time?" He looked at his friends expectantly. "We could grab dinner at the Blue Pearl."

Though Cai Long and Su Tao reacted differently than he had expected.

The blood rushed to Cai Long's face, rivaling his fiery red hair. As he was only wearing a leather apron over his trousers at work, Li Yuanjun could see the blush spreading over his neck, shoulders, and arms.

The exact opposite seemed to be happening to Su Tao. His bronze-colored skin turned an unhealthy gray, and his nostrils quivered as he drew in a deep breath.

When neither of them replied to his proposal, Li Yuanjun tried again. "It's about Weimin and my feelings . . . I mean Weimin's emotional life, of course. Right, we have to talk about Weimin because I am worried about him."

Cai Long gave him a confused look but gradually regained his normal skin color. Su Tao, who had been leaning on the counter behind him, expelled the air he had been holding. *Good*, Li Yuanjun thought, they hadn't noticed the slip of his tongue.

Su Tao seemed to have regained his composure first. "Yuanjun, what have you done now?" he wanted to know.

Li Yuanjun raised his hands in a helpless gesture. "What makes you think I could have done something wrong? Oh, let's forget about that for now. I will explain everything to you later. See you guys at the Blue Pearl in half an hour."

Without waiting for an answer, he turned around and left his friends speechless.

After passing by his house to leave the jug of wine, Li Yuanjun made his way to the Blue Pearl.

When he arrived, Su Tao and Cai Long waved at him. They had reserved a table in a quiet corner. With a hand gesture, he showed them that they should wait a little longer.

Li Yuanjun held back a student who had finished his meal and was about to leave. He told him to go round to He Weimin's house to bring him his dinner. He didn't want to burden He Weimin with his presence today. At least, that was what he tried to make himself believe. In reality, he was afraid of how He Weimin would receive him. He wanted to postpone this challenge until tomorrow.

When he arrived at his friends' table, Su Tao motioned for him to sit on one of the two free chairs opposite them. As he complied with the request, he had the feeling that he was about to be interrogated.

Before he could say anything, Lai Meixiu appeared at their table.

"The dish of the day is venison stew with carrot vegetables and rice," she said and prepared to take the order.

Li Yuanjun's stomach turned at the very thought of food. To avoid unnecessary questions, he ordered a portion anyway.

"What happened? Did you run out of mushrooms?" he couldn't resist asking Lai Meixiu.

"Enlai slept all night," she replied. "Mother was so happy this morning that she felt like cooking something special. Let's hope our lucky streak continues. What can I get you to drink? How about a Sweet Kiss?" she asked, without taking her eyes off Li Yuanjun.

"Anything but a Sweet Kiss. I have already had enough of those today. Get me a beer instead," he said with a warning look in Lai Meixiu's direction.

After she had also taken Su Tao and Cai Long's order, she looked around the dining room. "Where did you leave He Weimin? I thought you two were inseparable now," she asked Li Yuanjun.

"Not here," he stated the obvious and made a shooing motion with his hand.

Su Tao and Cai Long had been watching the conversation like a particularly exciting match of a board game. When Lai Meixiu turned round and disappeared toward the kitchen, they both started talking at the same time.

"What is this all about?" Su Tao wanted to know.

"Did you have a fight with Weimin?" asked Cai Long.

In response, Li Yuanjun lowered his head onto the fortunately clean table. Why couldn't he just wake up, and it'd turn out it was all just a dream? He lifted his head from the table and looked into two pairs of questioning eyes instead.

Li Yuanjun remembered that he was the one who wanted to talk to his friends, not the other way around. Hanging his head, he told Su Tao and Cai Long what had happened between him and He Weimin over the past few days. At first, the words came slowly, but then they just bubbled out of him. He ended with what had happened at the glade, the kiss, to be precise. Yet, he left his disturbing thoughts about his love life out of it for the moment.

"So you were exercising at the glade, and then you disappeared into the bushes to make out," Cai Long summarized when Li Yuanjun had finished his story.

Before Li Yuanjun could say anything in reply, Lai Meixiu brought their order. His revelations did not stop his friends from eating. As usual, Cai Long had been given an extra large portion, which was also necessary to keep his dragon body intact. The two seemed to have processed their shock from the smithy.

Su Tao gulped down a mouthful of meat and washed it down with a sip of wine—a Sweet Kiss. "This is delicious, finally meat again. Don't you want anything to eat?" he turned to Li Yuanjun.

"I am going to wait until it's cooled down a bit," Li Yuanjun lied. His stomach seemed to have knotted up into one of those knots that only sailors could do. Why weren't his friends more shocked by his experiences?

"What's the matter? You don't have anything to say about what happened?" Li Yuanjun couldn't stand waiting any longer. "Overall, Weimin is your friend, too. Surely you must have an opinion?"

Cai Long put his fork aside and slowly dabbed his mouth with one of the cloths provided. "I really cannot see what the problem is. I would argue that each of us has taken a conquest to this glade in order to spend some time apart from the students."

"I don't know," Li Yuanjun had to concede. "I had completely forgotten about the existence of the glade until the day before yesterday and was surprised that it was still there at all." He took a sip of his beer to distract from the untouched food.

"The kids don't call it the kissing glade for nothing," Su Tao said with his mouth full.

Li Yuanjun almost choked on his beer at the term *kissing*.

"It's really not that easy to find anything like privacy at the Yaosen," continued Cai Long, unperturbed. "Especially when everyone thinks they can enter each other's homes as they please . . ."

Cai Long fell silent when Su Tao elbowed him in the side. "Excuse me, go on," he said to Cai Long with narrowed brows and an icy stare.

Li Yuanjun considered the behavior of his two friends more than just weird. He had been right in his earlier observations. Something had been going on between them recently. He was obviously excluded from this 'something.'

To get back to the actual topic, he said, "What does that even mean—making out? There was no mention of making out."

In response, Cai Long merely made kissing noises between some bites of venison stew.

"By the way, that's not the point at all," Li Yuanjun huffed. "Did you even listen to me?" He had started to push the beer mug in circles on the table in order to give his hands something to do.

Su Tao rolled his eyes and pushed his plate forward so that he could rest his hands on the table. "We understood every single word," he said with a serious expression. "After the duel, Weimin gave you a kiss. Because you sat there speechless like a dreamy schoolgirl, the poor man had to crawl into bed alone today." The last words were already turning into laughter, and he continued to devote himself to his food.

"You aren't taking me seriously at all," Li Yuanjun complained and straightened up with a jerk, spilling some of his beer. "The problem isn't the kiss or that Weimin is lonely. This isn't even true, by the way, because he doesn't live alone. I practically forced him to give me a kiss."

When his friends fell silent, he added, "I don't even know if he likes men or is interested in romance at all."

"Let us start from the beginning," intervened Cai Long, who had now finished his meal and was leaning back in his chair. "He Weimin is not a helpless virgin." He faltered. "Anyway, he's not helpless. I would rather not speculate about the rest. He is a grown man of almost forty years. I am convinced he wouldn't have agreed to the bet if he didn't want the kiss."

"You think so?" Li Yuanjun asked, full of hope.

"Weimin could have refused to kiss you," continued Cai Long. "It is not like you tied him up and forced him."

Li Yuanjun had not yet considered the matter from this perspective. "Maybe Weimin did want the kiss a little," he encouraged himself. "Perhaps he also wanted to try out what it's like to kiss a man." He gave his friends a hopeful look.

The next thought made him pale and tilt his head toward the table. "I failed across the board," he stated. "The kiss was so bad that it sent Weimin running."

Cai Long placed one of his huge hands on Li Yuanjun's shoulder.

"Was it nice?" asked Su Tao, who had now emptied his plate of every last carrot.

"Weimin ran away. How could it have been nice for him?" asked Li Yuanjun absently.

"I mean, did *you* like the kiss?" Su Tao corrected him.

"What?" Li Yuanjun raised his eyebrows. "How could I not have liked it? Weimin is considerate and attractive, and you wouldn't believe how soft his lips feel when he doesn't pinch them together. Being kissed by him can only be pleasurable." Remembering the kiss, he wrapped his arms around his torso and closed his eyes. "Well, it could have been a bit longer and more intense, but . . ."

"There is that face again," Lai Meixiu, who had stepped up to the table unnoticed by him to clear the empty crockery, interrupted him.

Li Yuanjun lifted a hand to his face, only to feel the grimace of a lovesick fool. The shock hit him so hard that he slumped down in his chair. He rocked back and forth to calm himself down.

Lai Meixiu collected the crockery. "Aren't you going to do anything?" she asked Su Tao and Cai Long, who just sat there and stared at him wordlessly. With these words, she turned around and disappeared as quietly as she had come.

Li Yuanjun raised his head to look at the smiling faces of his so-called friends. Su Tao gently nudged Cai Long with his shoulder and gave him a prompting look.

"I think we have made Yuanjun suffer long enough," Su Tao said. "We should relieve him of his worries."

Chapter 12

THE WHOLE TRUTH

"Are you sure Weimin doesn't know the wine's name?" Cai Long wanted to know from Li Yuanjun.

Li Yuanjun had started to draw circles with his finger in the pool of beer on the table. He took some time to answer.

"I assumed that he must have heard that name. After all, it's the most popular drink in this region, and I have seen Weimin drinking it a few times myself." To avoid having to look at his friends, he connected the beer circles into a pattern. "Obviously, I was wrong. Weimin can't know the name, or he wouldn't have kissed me, obviously."

Satisfied with his reasoning, Li Yuanjun lifted his head to meet two pairs of eyes that were doing their best to avoid looking in his direction.

"Roughly a fortnight ago, we had dinner here with Weimin, and he ordered a Sweet Kiss," Su Tao broke the silence.

Li Yuanjun had to process this information first. He took a sip of what was left of his beer. Then he pushed his still full plate to the center of the table so that he didn't have to keep looking at it.

"Hold on, that can't be true." He thought he had caught his friend in a lie. "Weimin eats alone in his lodgings every evening. After all, I must know because I deliver his food every day."

Li Yuanjun leaned back in his chair and waited to see what his friends would say.

Cai Long began to slowly pull Li Yuanjun's untouched plate in his direction. When Su Tao noticed and tapped his finger on the table in warning, Cai Long lowered his hand with a guilty look and hid it under the table.

"That may be true when you're here, but we usually eat here with Weimin while you're traveling," Cai Long admitted.

Li Yuanjun had not expected this turn of events. When he thought about it, he realized that he hadn't been at the Yaosen School for several days a few weeks ago. About a fortnight ago, he had been traveling with some of the older students to a village where a poltergeist had been causing trouble. They had stayed in the village until the problem was resolved.

"Weimin is leading a double life," Li Yuanjun stated with a face of no emotions. "And you two have known about it all along," he accused the two sitting at the table with him, who had previously been his friends.

"On the way back from the Blue Pearl, we drop him off at his apartment, but that doesn't mean he wouldn't be able to make the journey on his own without any problems," Su Tao added salt to the wound.

"So Weimin knew the name of the wine, but did he also know its meaning?" Li Yuanjun grasped at one last straw.

"I would be very surprised if he didn't," Cai Long took away his last hope. "Weimin asked us the names of the wines that day, and we told him the story of the Blue Pearl couple." His hand came out from under the table to pull the plate a little further in his direction.

"Go on, tell the whole story before Li Yuanjun loses his patience," Su Tao urged him. "And please take your hands off my dessert," he added, looking at Li Yuanjun's plate.

Just like being in a trance, Li Yuanjun pushed his unused cutlery across the table. Nonetheless, food should never go to waste.

"Well, maybe we persuaded Weimin to join us for a wine tasting," Cai Long hurried to say. "He should have tasted each of the wines once, now that he's been able to give them a name."

"You wouldn't believe what the man can take before he gets drunk." Su Tao paid his respects to the absent He Weimin. "Yet, he cannot compete with Cai Long's skills and the dragons' alcohol tolerance."

Li Yuanjun swallowed hard. "You had your fun with Weimin and got him drunk. And you didn't invite me along. I hope you accompanied Weimin home safely afterward."

"Not quite," Su Tao confessed, popping one of the steamed carrots he had snatched from the plate into his mouth. "Long asked Weimin if he would like to eat with us more often. Weimin declined without hesitation, saying that you would then no longer bring him his food."

Li Yuanjun felt the urge to drop his head onto the tabletop. But it was full of spilled beer. He looked around the dining room. Where was Lai Meixiu with her wiping cloth when she was needed?

A butterfly seemed to have formed in Li Yuanjun's stomach. He Weimin had not wanted to hurt him by admitting that he no longer needed help from others. As with their training, He Weimin must have realized how much this time spent together meant to him.

He sat up straight and resolved that he would apologize to He Weimin tomorrow with all due courtesy.

"... Partner or wife ..."

Li Yuanjun just realized that his thoughts had wandered, and he had not followed the conversation. Had the drunken He Weimin revealed something about his past? Had he been married, or was he still? Li Yuanjun's stomach tightened, and he felt really sick now. Was there perhaps a woman and children waiting somewhere for He Weimin to return?

"What about He Weimin's wife? I hope she's alright?" he asked in a low voice, hoping his friends hadn't noticed his mental absence. The look that spread across their faces indicated the opposite, though.

"What are you talking about?" Cai Long's question came before Su Tao's, who had stuffed his mouth full of rice. "Weimin was surprised that you spent so much time dropping in on him and asked us if your wife or mistress wouldn't mind."

Su Tao swallowed his food. "The poor guy was already pretty down the drain at the time, daring to ask about your love life so obviously," he added.

At the term *love life*, Li Yuanjun winced and almost knocked over his beer mug. "What did you say to him?" he wanted to know.

"The truth, of course," Cai Long said with his mouth full and surprisingly intelligible. "You are as free as the wind and couldn't even maintain a romantic relationship if your life depended on it."

Li Yuanjun's jaw dropped. "I have had relationships. Nobody has complained."

"Exactly," Su Tao pointed out the obvious. "You don't say no to anyone, and then you let them go without resistance when losing interest."

"You just made that up to annoy Weimin," he accused his friends.

Cai Long raised a hand, and Su Tao enumerated, "The widow with the four children." Cai Long raised a finger in the air, "The librarian with the huge breasts . . . uhm . . . with the huge glasses." A second finger lifted. "The baker who was so lonely after his partner died." Three fingers . . . "Smug and Knack, the water spirits." Two more fingers.

Li Yuanjun interrupted the farce by bending one of the fingers back again. "Their names are Smaq and Kniq, and they are water gods."

"So the rumor is true," Su Tao rejoiced, "you had a relationship with both of them at the same ti—"

Li Yuanjun put his hand over Su Tao's mouth to stop him from continuing. "They are twins," he hissed as if that explained everything.

Su Tao raised his hands to signal his surrender until Li Yuanjun removed his hand from his mouth.

"You see where we're going with this," Cai Long said, squirming uncomfortably in his chair. "We've suspected for a while that Weimin has an interest in you. But since you didn't do anything, we thought you were deliberately ignoring it in order not to encourage him."

Li Yuanjun tried to control his breathing but only managed to let out a horrified gasp.

"You really didn't notice," Su Tao stated, his eyes almost popping out of his head in disbelief.

"Maybe I gave Weimin a little encouragement to try his luck with you after his near confession," Cai Long admitted meekly, rubbing his head.

"What did you say to him?" Li Yuanjun wanted to know in a calm voice.

"Well," Cai Long began, looking in every direction but Li Yuanjun's. "To begin with, he could give you a kiss to see where it leads."

"So?" Li Yuanjun tapped his foot impatiently on the floor.

"Then Weimin slumped down and slipped off his chair. I was allowed to carry not one but two drunks home that evening. But what surprises me most is that Weimin can still remember anything about that evening. I guess he can take more than I gave him credit for."

Li Yuanjun remained speechless. A state that didn't happen often but that had almost become the norm that evening. "So you think Weimin might like me, too?" he finally managed to say.

Su Tao waved a hand in front of Li Yuanjun's face. "I always thought it was a rumor. But it seems to be true that love turns even the greatest seducer into an idiot," he said. "Look at this face." He turned to Cai Long.

"True love turns everyone into an idiot," Cai Long repeated with a serious expression.

A week ago, heck, even yesterday, Li Yuanjun would have laughed at his friends for making such a remark. Once he had admitted his feelings to himself, it was no longer so difficult to accept them. The really hard work still lay ahead of him. He had to convince He Weimin that his feelings were sincere and hope that they were reciprocated.

With a jerk, Li Yuanjun straightened up from his chair, causing his friends to flinch in shock. "Enough to drink for today," he announced, looking at his still half-full beer mug. "I have to prepare for an important fight to conquer the love of my life."

Su Tao and Cai Long, who had been expecting a telling-off, stared at him as if he'd suddenly grown two heads.

"You will understand when you're in the same position," Li Yuanjun added. "The drinks are on me, apologize to Lai Meixiu on my behalf for the spilled beer. Wish me luck."

Li Yuanjun stood up and left the Blue Pearl with his head held high.

Chapter 13

Decisions

Li Yuanjun switched from one foot to the other. When he realized that he looked like a child with the urge to pee, he forced himself to stand still. He couldn't remember how he had gotten home yesterday or to the training ground in the morning.

The students seemed to have already become accustomed to his absent-minded behavior, as only children and teenagers could. At least they had stopped giving him questioning looks.

Today, nothing seemed to be going according to plan in class, which at least temporarily ensured that his thoughts didn't constantly drift off to He Weimin.

At first, two of the female students had argued about which of them was allowed to practice sword fighting with one of the older boys. The argument had not been about who had the best training partner. Both girls were far superior to their classmate in terms of their skills and would have been better off practicing together.

To smooth things over, Li Yuanjun promised that each of the students would be allowed to practice with the older one for as long as she wanted. With any luck, at least one of his students would learn something during training. Even if it was just not to make eyes at their classmates.

While Li Yuanjun was still congratulating himself on solving this problem, one of the younger boys injured himself with his own weapon. Fortunately, the injuries were not serious. However, Li Yuanjun wasted a lot of time trying to find Wan Zemin, the Yaosen healer. As usual, Wan Zemin had lost track of time while gathering medicinal herbs, and by the time Li Yuanjun found him, it was already afternoon.

Li Yuanjun finally managed to finish the lesson a little late. He secured the practice area and grabbed Bastard and the jug of Sweet Kiss, which seemed to be slowly becoming his constant companion.

With long strides, he made his way to the glade. Li Yuanjun could only hope that He Weimin was waiting for him if he had come to the clearing at all today.

The closer he got, the slower Li Yuanjun's steps became. The confidence he had felt last night was increasingly overshadowed by doubts. He wondered whether He Weimin was interested in him as a partner or whether he was misinterpreting his behavior again.

Perhaps He Weimin just wanted to see what it felt like to kiss a man and did not want a committed relationship. This thought hurt more than Li Yuanjun would have considered possible.

Li Yuanjun wondered what he hoped to get out of a romantic relationship with He Weimin. He stopped, took a deep breath, and closed his eyes. The images his mind showed him made his mouth go dry and his legs go soft.

He saw more innocent kisses and less innocent activities, preferably done naked. But there were also scenes that stubbornly pushed their way to the forefront.

He Weimin telling one of his stories while Li Yuanjun, who had his head in his lap, listened. Li Yuanjun reading a book to He Weimin on a snowy winter's day. The vision of the two of them sitting old and hunched over a game board in a room that looked suspiciously like his living room sent a pleasant shiver down Li Yuanjun's spine. Li Yuanjun had been meaning to buy one of these sensory games for some time.

However, a wrinkled He Weimin would not be here at the Yaosen but with his own clan. In a few months, he would be able to resume his old life. Li Yuanjun wanted to prevent He Weimin from turning his back on him and the Yaosen, so he had to act now.

He took a few deep breaths in and out to give himself courage for what was to come. Then he stood up and walked the few steps to the clearing without hesitation.

When Li Yuanjun found the glade deserted, a numbness spread through his limbs, which only subsided when he saw movement out of the corner of his eye. He Weimin was sitting by the oak tree and had been waiting for him.

"It's me, Li Yuanjun," he greeted He Weimin so as not to startle him.

After his feet regained their feeling, Li Yuanjun walked toward He Weimin, who stood up and held something in his outstretched hand. When Li Yuanjun got close enough, he recognized that it was a jug.

"I've brought your victory prize. Although it is already late, there should still be enough time for a competition," He Weimin said with an expressionless face.

He Weimin wanted to pretend that the kiss had never happened and carry on as before. Li Yuanjun decided to go along with He Weimin's behavior and confront him with the facts later.

"Agreed," Li Yuanjun reacted to He Weimin's suggestion. "I have also brought a jug of wine for the winner. The jugs can wait here in the shade for our return."

And if my plan goes wrong, at least I can get really drunk afterward, he added in his mind.

He Weimin put down the jug and turned to walk to the center of the clearing without another word. When Li Yuanjun saw how confidently He Weimin walked along the now familiar path, a dull feeling spread through his chest. It confirmed to him that He Weimin did not really need his help anymore.

As they prepared for battle and took up their positions, Li Yuanjun managed to suppress these thoughts.

Both cultivators were more familiar with each other's fighting techniques. Soon, a rapid exchange of attack and defense developed, requiring Li Yuanjun's full attention. He thought again that He Weimin, despite his blindness, would soon be able to hold his own against a real opponent. Especially with a partner by his side, he should hardly be limited.

Li Yuanjun realized that he could not defeat He Weimin a second time using the same tactics as the day before. In a real fight, he would try to distract his opponent in order to land a hit. He didn't want to use such a method against He Weimin, but in war and love, anything went.

Thinking about love, Li Yuanjun hesitated for a moment, which was enough for He Weimin to almost land a hit on his arm. He shook his head. If he still wanted to win the fight, he couldn't afford to let his concentration slip.

"Weimin, I have an idea," Li Yuanjun began a diversionary maneuver. "What do you say we raise the stakes?" Before He Weimin could reply, he continued, "How about a trip to paradise for the winner?"

To Li Yuanjun's credit, He Weimin managed to hide his surprise well. Only a slight tremor in his sword hand and the shifting of his weight to the right side revealed that the mention of the wine had had an effect. He took advantage of the weakness to launch a direct attack on He Weimin's left side.

Before Li Yuanjun's sword could find its target, a touch on his stomach stopped him in his tracks. When he looked down at himself, he saw the cause. It was the hilt of a dagger that He Weimin was holding in his left hand.

He Weimin had also resorted to trickery and slipped the weapon out of the sleeve of his coat, unnoticed by Li Yuanjun. He Weimin took a step back, skillfully turned the dagger in his hand, and slipped it back into his sleeve.

Li Yuanjun laughed out loud. "Very skillful indeed," he paid tribute to He Weimin. "This time, the victory definitely goes to you. I didn't expect such a move."

"Unfortunately, you can't use it several times against the same opponent," He Weimin conceded. "Without the dagger, I wouldn't have stood a chance against you. I won't have it so easy next time."

"Let's go to the shade," Li Yuanjun said.

He Weimin nodded and set off in the direction of their favorite resting place. Li Yuanjun followed slowly, lost in thought. It pained him that He Weimin didn't let him lead like before.

Like a teenager pulling his sweetheart by the pigtail to get her attention, Li Yuanjun couldn't resist teasing, "I'm already looking forward to finding out what other secrets you might have."

Li Yuanjun couldn't see He Weimin's expression, but the sight of his blushing ears sent a warm feeling through his body. *The blush is at least a step up from yesterday's paleness*, Li Yuanjun thought, resisting the temptation to kiss He Weimin so as not to scare him away.

He Weimin walked on without saying anything, only his hand tightened around his sword.

"So you're ambidextrous. Is it innate, or did you learn it later on?" Li Yuanjun broke the silence before it was about to become awkward. "I can defend myself to some extent with my left hand if necessary, but that's about it," he added.

"I was born this way," He Weimin replied without turning round. "My uncle first noticed it when we played together as children. Later, he taught me silly tricks, much to my parents' annoyance," he added, not quite able to keep the longing out of his voice.

"Weimin, why don't we walk the rest of the way together? It's tedious talking to your back."

He Weimin's steps slowed down until he stopped completely. Satisfied with himself, Li Yuanjun grabbed the bent arm that He Weimin held out to him.

"Was your ambidexterity the reason you trained with your uncle after he lost his hand?" Li Yuanjun asked, trying to get He Weimin to keep talking.

They set off together. "Yes and no," He Weimin replied and began to explain. "In the beginning, it was an advantage for my uncle to train with someone who could wield his weapon with his left hand. But I think it was also important for him that I learned to fight equally well with both hands. An unexpected change of weapon hand can mean the difference between victory and defeat in a fight."

"The oak tree is about two meters in front of us," said Li Yuanjun. "Shall we sit down or take another lap around the tree?"

"You're impossible," said He Weimin, the corners of his mouth almost turning up into a smile.

"And yet you like it," Li Yuanjun said in a calm voice.

"Whatever you say," was all He Weimin said in reply.

Li Yuanjun picked up the wine jugs and placed them within easy reach before sitting down next to He Weimin with an inelegant plop. He noticed that He Weimin had forgotten to spread his cloth underneath him. He was probably not as relaxed as he wanted to appear.

"Your dagger emits an energy. Is it a magical weapon?" Li Yuanjun wanted to know.

"You're right," He Weimin confirmed, "I got it during a quest. After I took over Sword, it became my main weapon."

"Surely such dexterity with your hands isn't only an advantage in battle?" Li Yuanjun couldn't resist teasing He Weimin.

"If you say so. I think we have earned some refreshment now." He Weimin avoided the challenge.

"But before we drink the wine, you should get your reward first," Li Yuanjun said and stood up. He had already devised a plan to prevent He Weimin from escaping again. Without warning, Li Yuanjun sat down frontally on He Weimin's lap, who was so surprised he couldn't utter a word.

"Get ready for your trip to paradise. You have earned it."

Chapter 14

Paradise

When He Weimin made no attempt to push Li Yuanjun back, he took this as consent. He leaned forward a little to touch He Weimin's mouth very gently with his lips and immediately withdrew again.

He Weimin did not move yet. As Li Yuanjun scanned his counterpart's face for a reaction, He Weimin opened his mouth to run the tip of his tongue over his lips as if to trace the kiss.

Noticing this, Li Yuanjun relaxed and repeated the kiss, applying a little more pressure now. He hadn't been wrong yesterday. He Weimin's lips were soft and warm.

Li Yuanjun barely managed to stop himself from cupping He Weimin's head with his hands and pulling him closer. He didn't want He Weimin to feel uncomfortable and to have the opportunity to pull away at any time.

To give his hands something to hold on to, Li Yuanjun leaned on the oak tree to He Weimin's right and left. He leaned back a little and looked He Weimin in the face. He Weimin's eyes were closed, and his lips were slightly parted as if in invitation.

Li Yuanjun resisted the urge to deepen the kiss and instead placed light kisses on He Weimin's eyelids. When he noticed how He Weimin relaxed, he first placed a kiss on the left corner of his mouth, then on the right. The temptation was too great; the tip of his nose also got a kiss, which was only fair, after all.

"Uhmm..." He Weimin tried to object.

Obviously, Li Yuanjun hadn't done a good enough job if He Weimin was still able to speak.

Li Yuanjun groped for He Weimin's hands and wrapped his arms around his hips. After a moment of hesitation, He Weimin tightened his grip, which made Li Yuanjun feel warm inside.

Inspired by this, Li Yuanjun dared to stroke He Weimin's lower lip with the tip of his tongue. He Weimin responded as he had hoped by opening his mouth slightly.

Li Yuanjun took this as an invitation to continue and slowly felt his way forward with his tongue. He wanted to prevent He Weimin from pushing him away in fright. It was certainly not his intention to land on his back like this.

When Li Yuanjun pushed forward into He Weimin's mouth with a little more force, the latter flinched slightly. He immediately retreated. "Take it easy. We won't do anything you don't like, and you set the pace. As soon as something makes you uncomfortable, you say so, and I'll stop."

"More," was all He Weimin replied before he pulled Li Yuanjun closer to him and searched for a way into his open mouth with his tongue.

A pleasant emptiness spread through Li Yuanjun's mind as his blood was needed more urgently elsewhere. The next thing Li Yuanjun was consciously aware of was a series of light kisses that He Weimin spread on his neck, eliciting a sigh from him. At some point, Li Yuanjun must have lifted himself off He Weimin's lap so that He Weimin's hands were no longer on his hips but on his bum.

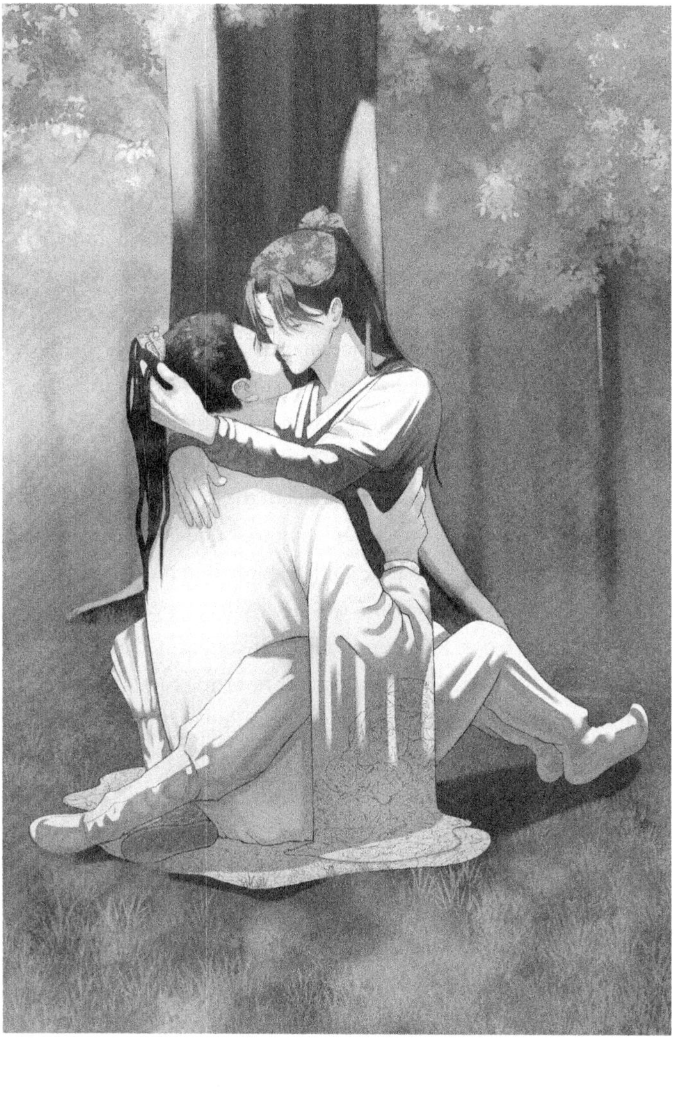

When He Weimin's hands lightly squeezed his buttocks, Li Yuanjun made an encouraging sound. The light squeeze showed Li Yuanjun that it was not accidental but that He Weimin knew what he was doing. He pushed himself toward He Weimin's hands, then settled on him again and rubbed against him.

When Li Yuanjun lowered himself onto He Weimin's lap again, he realized with satisfaction that the latter's relaxation had not lasted. Some parts of He Weimin's body were anything but relaxed now. Li Yuanjun leaned his arms on the oak tree behind He Weimin and was about to intensify his efforts when a last remnant of his mind reminded him that he actually wanted to *talk* to He Weimin.

Before his mind could finally fail him, Li Yuanjun pressed a quick kiss to He Weimin's mouth and then moved his lips to his ear. To delay the inevitable for as long as possible, he ran the tip of his tongue along the shell of He Weimin's ear, causing him to shudder. Li Yuanjun had to memorize this spot so that he could explore it in more detail later.

"Why did you pretend not to know what Sweet Kiss is?" Li Yuanjun whispered in He Weimin's ear. "If you wanted a real kiss, all you had to do was ask. Shame on you for resorting to such a ruse."

Hearing this, He Weimin froze before leaning back as far as the oak tree would allow and trying to push Li Yuanjun off his lap. The latter had already expected a similar reaction and crossed his legs behind He Weimin's back.

"Today, I won't let you go until we've talked," Li Yuanjun promised.

He Weimin stopped trying to escape and lowered his arms to the ground in resignation. "I am sorry," he confessed. "It wasn't my intention to deceive you—at least not at first." His voice got softer and softer, so Li Yuanjun would hardly have understood him.

Li Yuanjun loosened his grip slightly without letting go of He Weimin completely. "I am not sorry," he announced. "If you hadn't made the first move, we'd be sneaking around each other like two schoolboys for all eternity. I still can't believe I misjudged your behavior like that."

"How did you find out?"

"It may shock you to hear, but Tao and Long can't keep secrets."

"Oh, the wine evening," He Weimin just said, trying to hide his expression by lowering his head.

Li Yuanjun carefully grabbed He Weimin's hands, which had dug into the grass. "You can tell me everything in peace. If you prefer, feel free to lean on my shoulder."

He Weimin remained sitting upright but loosened his grip on the grass and intertwined his fingers with Li Yuanjun's. "I didn't want you to notice any of this. I was planning to leave the Yaosen in a few months and take the memories of you with me."

Li Yuanjun focused on the essence of He Weimin's confession. "You say you were planning to. Does that mean you don't want to leave now?"

"That's not what I meant. To tell you the truth, I don't know what I want my future to look like." After a moment's hesitation, he added in a raspy voice, "However, there is one more thing I have to do first."

When He Weimin didn't continue, Li Yuanjun decided to leave the matter alone for the time being.

"Are you more attracted to men, or do you, like me, not care about the gender of your partners?"

He Weimin was suddenly struck by the question. He let go of Li Yuanjun's hands and wanted to turn his face away. Then, he apparently remembered Li Yuanjun's words and leaned against Li Yuanjun's shoulder.

"I am not sure," He Weimin replied, "but I have never felt the same way about women as I do about men."

Li Yuanjun caught a whiff of He Weimin's unmistakable soap scent. He realized that this was the first time he had hugged He Weimin. To distract himself from his feelings, he started rubbing

He Weimin's back. "That is not important. Everyone decides for themselves who they love . . . uhm, who they're attracted to."

"It is important for my family and the clan," said He Weimin, who had obviously missed the slip of the tongue. "Such behavior is tolerated to a certain extent among teenagers and young adults. However, the obligation to marry and start a family exists for everyone."

Li Yuanjun had to swallow hard. He didn't know if he wanted to hear the answer to his next question. "Your clan has strict social expectations," he stated. "Is there someone waiting for you, or did you have a wife?"

He Weimin tensed in his arms but did not retreat. "A fiancée," he finally managed to say in a low voice. "I was engaged, but we broke up before the wedding could take place."

A wave of relief washed over Li Yuanjun, but at the same time, he realized that this could not be the end of the story. "You don't have to tell me if you don't want to," he tried to reassure He Weimin.

"I think you have a right to hear the whole story," said He Weimin, who seemed to have regained his composure.

Li Yuanjun knew that talking about painful events could help. He resumed his stroking and gave He Weimin a light kiss on the cheek.

He Weimin returned the gesture, hitting Li Yuanjun's neck, eliciting a sigh from the latter.

Later; now it's Weimin's turn, he reminded himself.

He Weimin took a deep breath to brace himself for what was to come before he began his story.

"My uncle noticed early on that I was more attracted to boys than girls. I think he felt similarly, which is why he recognized himself in me. I didn't notice it at the time, but he always tried to shield us from the expectations of the family and the clan. He managed to do this for a while by taking me with him on his travels.

After he was wounded and returned to the family, we were left alone for a while. After my uncle was gone, my parents decided it was finally time for me to get married and start a family of my own.

The loss of my uncle had hit me hard, and I didn't have the strength to resist them. I was still able to politely decline the first marriage candidates they presented to me. However, my parents became increasingly impatient.

When the leader of our clan insisted on my engagement to one of his nieces, my parents gave me a choice. I was either to marry this barely twenty-year-old woman, whom I only knew by sight or leave the clan forever under some pretense that it would spare my parents the shame.

Hao Wenling is an attractive young woman from a prestigious family. Her cultivation skills are not strong, and her movement has been limited since a childhood accident. For these reasons, no man had ever shown a deeper interest in her.

I knew from the beginning that I would not be able to offer Hao Wenling anything other than my friendship in a marriage, but I was too cowardly to tell her directly.

My parents had already announced our engagement without my consent. As my fiancée, Hao Wenling was to spend the time until the wedding in my family home.

When I argued with my father one evening and demanded that he refuse the marriage, we were overheard by Hao Wenling. She must have thought I was rejecting her for her sake and fled, not caring that it was already dark outside."

He Weimin had dug his hands into Li Yuanjun's clothes. When he hesitated to continue, Li Yuanjun asked, "Was that when you became blind?"

"Yes," He Weimin confirmed, "I lost my vision that night."

Chapter 15
The Burdens Of The Past

Li Yuanjun didn't quite know what he could do to comfort He Weimin. He didn't want to let He Weimin out of his arms and hugged him a little tighter when he remembered the wine they had brought.

"How about a cup of wine?" he suggested. Perhaps that would calm He Weimin down a little. In any case, he himself needed some refreshment to listen to the story.

"Thank you," He Weimin accepted the offer.

As Li Yuanjun got up from his comfortable seat, he felt a pang of regret. Before he could deepen the thought, he reached for one of the waiting jugs and looked around for the cups that He Weimin had brought as a precaution.

Li Yuanjun poured a cup of wine and pressed it into He Weimin's hand. When he wanted to do the same for himself, he realized that he could no longer sit on He Weimin with the cup and involuntarily let out a sigh.

"What's wrong?" He Weimin wanted to know.

"My seat is gone, but it was so comfortable."

He Weimin had understood him and tapped the spot next to him with his free hand. "We can sit next to each other. I also promise not to run away," He Weimin said with a guilty look.

Li Yuanjun sat down on the grass next to He Weimin and moved closer to him until their upper arms were touching.

"Mhm, I won't let you off that easily," he promised and put his arm around He Weimin's waist.

Li Yuanjun drank a deep draught of the wine and leaned as close to He Weimin as he could. "Now I am ready for the continuation of your story," Li Yuanjun said and waited.

He Weimin took a sip of his wine, then a second. He leaned against Li Yuanjun and, after clearing his throat several times, began to speak.

"Her escape led Hao Wenling to an ancient burial mound on our clan's grounds. To prevent people from entering the tomb, stone tablets with a warning had been erected in every direction.

I don't know whether Hao Wenling overlooked the inscriptions or ignored them in her haste. She must have touched the earth on the grave, causing a vengeful spirit to be released."

He Weimin took another sip of wine, which Li Yuanjun took advantage of to ask a question. "What is this spirit you are harboring on your ground?"

Upon hearing this, He Weimin slumped noticeably. "The spirit was formed over a long period of time, and Hao Wenling allowed it to take shape for the first time.

"Over a century ago, we had a dog plague. The domesticated dogs had mated uncontrollably with a pack of semi-wild wolves. These wild dogs were more aggressive than their ancestors and became a danger to humans and their livestock. Targeted hunts organized by the clan chief at the time only provided temporary relief.

"As the situation continued to deteriorate, a bounty was offered for every wild dog killed. This offer attracted many dog catchers and dubious characters. At first, the plan seemed to work, and the bounty hunters were successful. However, these semi-wild creatures did not behave like ordinary dogs. As more and more of them were killed, the remaining ones formed a pack and attacked the hunters.

"One bounty hunter after another was killed in this way. It was only a matter of time before the dogs gained the upper hand.

"What followed was a cruel slaughter. All animals that remotely resembled a dog were killed. As a sign of their victory, the bounty hunters hung the carcasses of their prey from the trees by the hill. They chose this spot so that the dogs that had survived the slaughter could see them from a distance and be scared off.

After the hunters had left the area, the clan members did not dare to remove the bodies at first. It was only months later that a group of young cultivators agreed to enter the hill and bury the remains of the dogs in a mass grave.

"At the time, it was believed that the matter had been settled, and it actually remained quiet for the next century. At some point, the only reminder of the incident was the clan's ban on keeping dogs."

As the silence continued, Li Yuanjun felt obliged to say something. "Your clan's behavior, well . . ."

"It was irresponsible," He Weimin continued the thought. "I myself only learned the details afterward. We should have done something much earlier. The violent death of so many vengeful beings often leads to the emergence of evil spirits."

"You cannot solve problems by burying them deep in the ground," Li Yuanjun agreed. "Your ancestors must have believed that future generations would take care of them."

"Unfortunately, we haven't managed to do that yet," said He Weimin.

"Would you like some more wine?" asked Li Yuanjun, who had noticed that He Weimin's cup was empty.

"I would love some," said He Weimin and held out the cup to Li Yuanjun.

Li Yuanjun swirled the jug and realized that he must have drunk all the wine during He Weimin's story.

"Oops, that was all of it," he confessed to He Weimin. "Luckily, we still have a second jug." He fished for the full jug with his hand without leaving He Weimin's side.

Li Yuanjun filled He Weimin's cup but then closed the jug as a precaution so that he wouldn't be tempted to drink more.

"So your fiancée woke up the ghost?" Li Yuanjun picked up the thread of the story again.

He Weimin stiffened beside him. "She is not my fiancée," he clarified, triggering a warm feeling in Li Yuanjun.

"Hao Wenling's escape ended at this mass dog grave. The ghosts of the dogs had never found peace. Time had simply stood still for them. Just like then, when they were alive, they now joined together in death to take revenge on their murderers.

"When Hao Wenling touched the earth on the grave, the spirits of the slaughtered dogs wanted to appropriate her body as a vessel. Although her cultivation abilities were weak, she noticed the spirit's presence before it could completely take over her body. She still managed to send out a magical signal for help.

"I was the first to arrive at the burial site. Hao Wenling was already very weak from the loss of energy but still alive.

The spirit had already partially taken on the appearance of Hao Wenling. The upper body was a perfect copy of her. Instead of legs, the creature had countless dog-front bodies, each of which seemed to have a life of its own.

I tried to lure the spirit away from the unconscious Hao Wenling so that she wouldn't get hurt in the fight. The plan seemed to work at first, and I managed to cut off two of the dog heads with Sword.

Instead of blood, the wounds oozed an acidic liquid. I wasn't quick enough, so a splash of it hit me in the face."

He Weimin paused in his narration and tensed beside him. Li Yuanjun wordlessly filled his cup a third time and groped for He Weimin's with his free hand. He Weimin intertwined his fingers with Li Yuanjun's, which seemed to calm him down enough for him to continue his story.

"I was able to wipe the acid off in a makeshift manner, but some of it had already got into my eyes."

He Weimin wanted to touch his face with his hand, lost in memories, but then realized that Li Yuanjun was holding it.

"My vision started to blur, and I had to make a decision quickly. I could treat my injuries, but then the ghost would have killed Hao Wenling. Half-blind, I didn't stand a chance in battle either, so I stood in front of Hao Wenling to protect her and fend off the attacks.

"My family and clan members had followed the help signal to the scene of the battle. When they arrived, the ghost fled.

"Hao Wenling and I were brought back to our clan. She recovered from the loss of energy within a few days, but my eyesight deteriorated until I could no longer see, despite the efforts of our healer."

He Weimin told the rest of the story with an expressionless face as if it had happened to someone else and not to him. The only sign of how upset he was by the memories were the tears that were welling up under his closed eyelids.

Li Yuanjun took the half-full cup of wine from He Weimin's hand and turned to him. He first gave He Weimin a gentle kiss on the mouth and then one on each eyelid. He then pulled He Weimin into a hug, which He Weimin returned, first carefully, then more firmly.

"Was the battle I witnessed a few days ago against the spirit creature?" Li Yuanjun wanted to know.

"Yes, the events just won't let me go. I kept trying to figure out where I might have made a mistake. Although I've gone through dozens of different scenarios, I can't think of any way to change the outcome of the battle.

But the worst thing is that the ghost is still up to mischief. It must still be lingering near the tomb, probably waiting for a new victim whose body it can take over."

"Hasn't your clan done anything?"

He Weimin clenched his hands into fists. "Our clan leader decided to wait and see if the spirit returns to rest. The clan members have been warned not to enter the hill, but travelers are unaware of the danger and could be attacked."

"You don't agree with your clan's actions," Li Yuanjun stated.

"Correct. I will hunt down the ghost as soon as I am able."

"Is that why you came to the Yaosen? You want to prepare for this battle?" Li Yuanjun surmised, unable to suppress a tremor in his voice. He Weimin's plan sounded like a suicide mission to him.

"It wasn't my decision to come to the Yaosen," He Weimin said. "When it became clear that I would never be able to see anything again, my parents arranged the trip. They had heard rumors about a wise woman who was said to be able to cure all kinds of ailments."

Li Yuanjun frowned. "Although my grandmother is a powerful woman, she can't restore your eyesight. I don't think she concealed this from you when you arrived."

"Actually, she didn't. But Li Xifeng has offered to let me stay at the Yaosen School for as long as I want. She also promised to teach me some techniques that would make it easier for me to deal with my blindness."

Li Yuanjun needed to know if there was a place for him in He Weimin's life. Nevertheless, he feared the answer and did not dare to look He Weimin in the face when he spoke next, so he leaned on Weimin's shoulder.

"So you're planning to return to your clan soon and face the spirit creature? I'm sure your family and Hao Wenling will be happy to see you back, even if you can't see again."

Li Yuanjun could feel He Weimin shaking his head slightly. "I will return, but not for the sake of my family or Hao Wenling. The engagement was canceled before I left, which the clan members reluctantly accepted. I'm done with that part of my life, and this will be the last time I set foot on clan soil."

Li Yuanjun tightened his grip on He Weimin's waist so there was still hope that he wouldn't lose He Weimin forever.

"That sounds like a good plan," he approved. "However, I would suggest a small change. You shouldn't go alone. I will accompany you," he blurted out before he could stop himself.

Li Yuanjun had leaned back so that he could look He Weimin in the face. When He Weimin opened his mouth to say something, Li Yuanjun lost his courage and put a hand over He Weimin's mouth.

"I don't mean to belittle your skill," he hastened to say. "I am sure you could defeat the spirit on your own. After the practice battles, I've come to the conclusion that we make a good team in battle. Our skills complement each other perfectly..."

"You can stop trying to persuade me," said He Weimin, who had taken Li Yuanjun's hand from his mouth and placed it on his cheek instead. "If you want to keep spending time with me, all you have to do is say so. I would be happy if we could go on this adventure together. But then what will become of your work?"

Li Yuanjun felt a smile spread across his face. "What work?" he asked absent-mindedly.

"You teach the students swordplay. Would they be able to manage without you for a while?"

"Oh, *this* work. I'm by no means irreplaceable. Now that I think about it, it might even be of use to Xue Mengyao."

"I don't understand."

"Your two roommates should slowly become full-fledged members of the school. Dai Liuxian already works as a stable master and helps out in the smithy. Xue Mengyao is a good swordsman and will become a capable teacher one day. As long as the students have me, he can't prove himself. My absence will help him in this matter."

"You've already planned everything. How could I refuse? And I suppose we'll have to continue training together until we go on our adventure?"

"Well, training sounds good," Li Yuanjun murmured contentedly against He Weimin's neck and reached for the jug of wine. "Surely we want to keep the reward for the winner?" he wanted to know and thought about how he could take a sip of wine without letting go of He Weimin.

He Weimin remained silent for so long that Li Yuanjun thought he had misunderstood him again.

"No," He Weimin finally said and paused. "I am in favor of increasing the reward. What do you think of a double climax? We would both get something out of it."

Li Yuanjun, who was holding the wine jug, startled and almost poured the wine over them both. He Weimin's quick wit never ceased to amaze him.

"Weimin, I think you'll make a worthy partner in more ways than one."

Epilogue

A Double-Edged Sword

One month before...

He Weimin sat up in his bed with a jerk and did not know what had woken him up.

When the suppressed moaning was repeated, he initially thought he was in the hospital bed where he had spent the first few weeks after being wounded.

"Meng'er, you promised to be quieter. If you can't control yourself, you will wake Weimin up." He Weimin was called back to the present by a failed attempt at whispering.

He Weimin was in his dwelling at the Yaosen, which he shared with Xue Mengyao and Dai Liuxian. He breathed in and out deeply before carefully lowering his head onto his pillow so as not to make any noise. His heartbeat began to normalize as the bed in the other corner of the room made creaking noises, indicating that it was not designed for two adults.

"I am trying to be quiet," Xue Mengyao said at that moment, not quiet at all. "You should realize by now that I cannot stay quiet when you do that with your fingers." He dismissed all blame.

"What else am I supposed to use?" asked Dai Liuxian desperately. "The you-know-what is making those farting noises. Do you want Weimin to think we have chronic flatulence?"

"Maybe he cannot hear us," Xue Mengyao tried to reassure Dai Liuxian with a wheeze in his voice. "I think Weimin is in a deep sleep."

If only, He Weimin thought, burying his head in the pillow to muffle the sounds. By now, he wished he wasn't blind but deaf. Or perhaps both.

When his two roommates had started their nocturnal activities a few weeks ago, He Weimin initially thought he had misheard them. However, he soon had to admit to himself that the two of them really were doing what it sounded like they were doing.

The reason for moving the interpersonal activities indoors was, as He Weimin had involuntarily overheard, that it had become too uncomfortable to be constantly outside for some of the duo. The lack of certain accessories also contributed to this.

The couple, and they were undoubtedly a couple, had been trying to suppress the noises made during lovemaking ever since. Their efforts to be discreet were sometimes crowned with more, sometimes with less success. Tonight was clearly one of the failures when it came to lowering the noise level.

"Did you just bite me again?" Xue Mengyao wanted to know in a voice that wasn't really whispering.

"But Meng'er, I have to mark my territory."

"Keep your teeth off my neck in the future, or I will mark my territory by kicking your bum."

The two of them began to giggle, as only lovers who had completely forgotten the world around them could do. He Weimin pulled the duvet over his head, regardless of the summer heat, and tried to block out the noises through meditation.

Although the voices faded into the background, he was unable to fall asleep again. He Weimin's thoughts returned to the time of his arrival at Yaosen School almost a year ago . . .

HE WEIMIN, HIS FATHER He Wenyan, and He Ru, the youngest of his three brothers, had ridden all the way to Yaosen. They had only taken short breaks at night to give the horses some rest. After a week, He Weimin had given up counting the days and preferred to conserve his strength.

His left leg, which had a barely healed wound, had started to hurt again. He wanted to feel for it to check whether the wound had reopened. When he felt nauseous, he gave up the attempt and straightened up in his saddle.

He Weimin inhaled slowly and deeply through his nose. The smell of the wet forest ground left behind by yesterday's downpour helped him to banish the feeling of dizziness.

"We'll soon have made it," his father said. "After the next bend in the path, we should come across the Yaosen compound."

His brother, He Ru, quickened his stallion's pace, and He Weimin's mare followed him obediently as she had done the whole journey. Sweat gathered on the back of He Weimin's neck. Every sway of the horse's back reminded him that he was no longer able to fly on his sword. The journey would have been considerably shorter this way and would have saved his family a lot of time.

"I imagined the Yaosen to be more impressive," his brother announced. "It looks like a collection of simple wooden houses in the middle of the forest. It's hard to imagine that the clans and sects are so keen to house their sons and daughters here."

"Li Xifeng's reputation is unshattered," He Wenyan rebuked. "If she can't restore my son's vision, then no one can."

He Weimin flinched involuntarily at his father's words. He appreciated what his family had taken upon themselves to find a cure for him. He himself had come to terms with his blindness and wanted to get on with his life.

"The houses all look equally shabby," He Ru observed. "We should start with the single building on the plateau and ask for Li Xifeng there."

"Yes, let's start there," He Weimin's father decided. "Ru, you take the reins of your brother's mare. The path is uneven and runs alongside a river."

He Weimin would have liked to ask for a more detailed description of the surroundings, but he didn't want to remind his father and brother of his blindness unnecessarily. With a pounding heart, he let himself be guided and wondered what kind of reception they would receive.

If the school's finances were as bad as He Ru's description suggested, they certainly didn't need an extra eater, especially not one who was barely able to walk without help, let alone work. He Weimin's family was not poor, but he doubted that they would be willing to spend an enormous amount of money to cure him. He Weimin had a little savings of his own; perhaps they would let him stay until he could manage on his own.

He Weimin recognized from the increasing sound of water that they must now be near the river his father had spoken of. For He Ru, Yaosen might have been a poor village, but the area made a different impression on him.

A light breeze cooled his sweaty neck and brought with it the fresh smell of the river. The bright laughter of children made its way through the sounds of the water. A hammer hit an anvil, causing a horse in the distance to neigh and his mare to raise her head in curiosity. A hen announced with a loud cluck that she had just laid an egg. The smell of freshly baked bread made He Weimin's stomach growl and told him that, unbeknownst to him, midday had already turned into afternoon.

"We're here," He Ru announced, proving to He Weimin that the school grounds were indeed not very far away. When his mare had come to a halt, he got out of the saddle and ignored the feeling of weakness in his legs.

"You take care of the horses," He Wenyan turned to He Ru. "I'll go to the house with your brother."

He Weimin stepped from one foot to the other as he waited for his father to take him by the arm to lead him. He knew it made His Father uncomfortable as it constantly reminded him of his son's blindness.

As they slowly walked toward the house, a man's loud laughter interrupted the silence. This unaffected sound made He Weimin forget the hardships of the journey for a moment.

The opening of a door interrupted his thoughts. "Yuanjun, we have visitors. Why don't you put the tea water on while I greet them?"

"At your order, Grandmother," came the flippant but warm-hearted reply from inside the building.

"You must be exhausted from the long journey. Come into the house," a female voice welcomed them.

He Weimin couldn't shake off the feeling that they were already expected.

Li Xifeng, who had opened the door for them, led father and son into a room. She took the opportunity to lead He Weimin by the arm to a table surrounded by two armchairs and a sofa. To He Weimin's relief, Li Xifeng gave a brief description of the room before pushing him into one of the worn armchairs.

He Weimin was overwhelmed by all the new impressions and was glad that his father took over the talking. He sat up straight and sipped the tea that Li Yuanjun had pressed into his hand.

He Wenyan told Li Xifeng the reason for their journey, which was only right for He Weimin as he probably wouldn't have dared to ask for a cure directly. When Li Xifeng was satisfied with monosyllabic answers, he was already afraid that her request would be rejected.

"I would like to speak to He Weimin alone," Li Xifeng interrupted his father, who had just started to negotiate the price. He Weimin was so surprised that he almost missed the table when he tried to put his cup down.

After his blindness, people had started talking to his companions instead of him.

"Yuanjun, please see He Wenyan out," Li Xifeng added, addressing her grandson.

His father must have stood up because he put a hand on He Weimin's shoulder. "Do your best, son," he addressed him. He Weimin now felt even more like a student who had to take an exam.

After his father and Li Yuanjun had left the room, He Weimin didn't know what to do with his hands, so he folded them in his lap.

"Take it easy, young Weimin. What we discuss now is between us," Li Xifeng said, placing a hand on his arm. Knowing exactly where his dialogue partner was allowed him to relax.

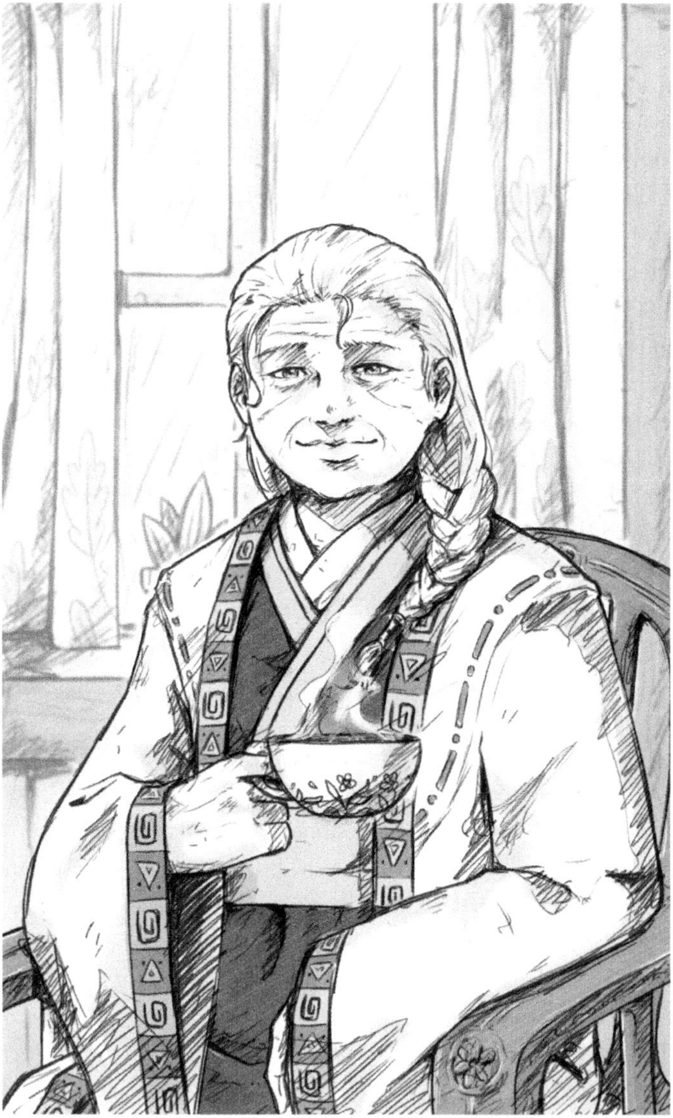

"The way I see it, my grandson's curiosity will soon bring him back," Li Xifeng let him know. "So we don't have much time to talk in peace. Let us get straight to the reason for your journey. As I've already heard from your father, you think you can get your vision back with my help?"

He Weimin was about to answer in the affirmative when something made him hesitate. Of course, he wanted to be able to see again, but that was not the reason why he had undertaken the journey. It was a new start, away from his family, as he secretly hoped.

He took a deep breath to brace himself for his answer. "No," He Weimin heard himself say. "I don't want to chase after a cure that probably doesn't exist. Forgive my bluntness, but although you have a lot of credibility, no one has ever said that you can restore sight to the blind."

Before Li Xifeng could reply, He Weimin hurried to add, "I am asking to be accepted into the Yaosen School."

"So you want to become a member of the school, even if you can never see again?" Li Xifeng made sure.

He Weimin straightened up in his seat. He had made his decision. "Yes," he confirmed. "I may be blind, but as far as my abilities allow, I will gladly put them at the service of the school."

"An excellent decision," He Weimin heard Li Xifeng say. "You will fit in well with our family," she added in a whisper so that He Weimin could not be sure he had heard her correctly.

"Excuse me?" he asked.

"You'll fit in well with the Yaosen," Li Xifeng readily answered, accompanied by a laugh. He had obviously misunderstood her when she had spoken about her family.

He Weimin heard the rustling of clothes as Li Xifeng stood up and touched him on the arm. "I will let your family know that I will do everything in my power to support you, and you can stay with us for as long as you want. That should satisfy your clan for now."

He Weimin was overwhelmed and could only manage a nod.

"Good, then it's a done deal," Li Xifeng confirmed. "Now you want to recover from the journey. My grandson will show you where you will be staying. Tomorrow, he can show you around Yaosen and introduce you to everyone. Isn't that right, Yuanjun?" she turned toward the entrance to the house.

"I certainly wasn't eavesdropping. I've only just returned," came the unconvincing attempt at a lie from Li Yuanjun's mouth.

"Of course not, that wouldn't suit you either," Li Xifeng saw through him. "And now you can lead He Weimin to the house of Xue Mengyao and Dai Liuxian, where he will live for now."

Li Xifeng addressed her next words to He Weimin, whose arm she hadn't let go of the whole time. "I will sort things out with your father. In the meantime, I will leave you in Yuanjun's care. You both seem to be the same age, and I think you'll be a good match. We will start your training tomorrow. Even if I can't cure your blindness, with your cultivation skills, it should be possible to replace your eyesight over time."

Before He Weimin could thank Li Xifeng, she rushed out of the room. A feeling of deep satisfaction spread through He Weimin. However, before his body could relax, a warm hand placed itself on his shoulder.

"And there she's gone," said Li Yuanjun. "Sometimes I think grandmother is not from this world. Now you have me. If you need anything, just let me know."

Li Xifeng turned out to be a strict but fair teacher. After just a few weeks, He Weimin was able to walk without a cane on familiar terrain.

At his insistence, Li Xifeng assigned him a job in the pharmacy. The owner of the pharmacy, the alchemist Deng Tingfeng, had then reluctantly accepted him as his apprentice. Although Deng Tingfeng must have been very old, he did not like being talked into his work and treated He Weimin like a superfluous object.

He Weimin had initially believed that the work was solely to make him feel useful. Now, more than half a year later, he could say that he had already learned more about alchemy than he had in his entire life. While he did simple tasks for Deng Tingfeng, such as cleaning the test tubes, the number of which seemed endless, the latter explained the basics of the craft to him.

He Weimin's life developed in a good direction, and a normal everyday life slowly began to emerge. He soon found two friends in Su Tao and Cai Long. Had it not been for the presence of Li Yuanjun, he would have felt completely at ease.

Soon after his arrival at the Yaosen, He Weimin had to admit to himself that he was about to fall in love with Li Yuanjun. Li Yuanjun, who always seemed to be in his neighborhood and had a smile for everyone.

He Weimin had initially believed that Li Yuanjun was looking after him at his grandmother's behest. He simply could not refuse the kind offer to bring him dinner every day. Li Yuanjun's arrival soon became the highlight of every day, and it was certainly not because of the admittedly delicious dishes.

To prevent Li Yuanjun from realizing his growing feelings, he tried to create more distance between them. To avoid giving himself away, He Weimin avoided talking to Li Yuanjun as much as possible.

He Weimin was torn inside. Although he wanted Li Yuanjun to stop his endeavors, he was also afraid of it. Li Yuanjun surprised He Weimin with his stubbornness.

The more He Weimin kept quiet, the more Li Yuanjun talked to him and sought his closeness. He Weimin could only hope that Li

Yuanjun would not realize his feelings for him. He would not be able to bear the aversion he would surely feel for him.

THE SQUEAKING OF BEDSPRINGS jolted He Weimin out of his memories. His two roommates had just started their second round of activities. He Weimin put his pillow over his ears and gave up the idea of sleep.

He used the time to think of a solution to his dilemma. When, what felt like an eternity later, the room was filled with the sound of contented snoring, He Weimin knew what he had to do. In the morning, he would tell his friendly but unfortunately noisy roommates that he would be resuming his weapons training. They should, therefore, not expect him to return before nightfall.

This should give them enough time to let off steam in the afternoon, and He Weimin could sleep in peace again at night. Satisfied with himself, he patted his pillow into shape and relaxed, turning onto his side to allow himself a few more hours of sleep.

PRESENT DAY...

He Weimin felt the hard bark of the oak against his back as Li Yuanjun pushed him against the tree. At some point, his legs must have given way under him because Li Yuanjun had shoved one of his muscular thighs between them to hold him upright.

Li Yuanjun had pushed He Weimin's hair to the side and kissed his way down his neck to the collar of his shirt. No, that wasn't true. The shirt was open, and Li Yuanjun had already reached his collarbone.

"Uhm, don't leave any marks," Li Yuanjun mumbled against He Weimin's neck. "If we don't sit down, your clothes won't get dirty, either. Don't worry, I will take care of it."

For the life of him, He Weimin didn't know what Li Yuanjun meant. He wouldn't have minded a few traces to prove that he wasn't just dreaming the events. The thing that just bumped against his hip was definitely not a dream, nor was it Li Yuanjun's sword: Bastard and Sword were lying on the ground next to them, where they had placed them some time ago.

To avoid being crushed between Li Yuanjun and the tree, He Weimin pressed himself towards Li Yuanjun. At least, that was how he justified his behavior to himself. Li Yuanjun rewarded him with a growl, as he seemed to have lost the ability to speak in complete sentences.

"Your hair thingy is in the way," Li Yuanjun muttered, proving him wrong.

He Weimin released one of his hands, which he had clasped in Li Yuanjun's shirt, to loosen the clip in one fluid movement and let it disappear into his sleeve.

"Better," came Li Yuanjun's confirmation, and he ran a hand through the strands of He Weimin's hair that had come loose. "What is that smell?" he wanted to know.

"Should I wash myself?" He Weimin mumbled, embarrassed. "We've hardly trained, but with the warmth of the summer . . ."

"Don't wash," Li Yuanjun said into his hair. "I thought the scent that always clings to you comes from your soap. But it's just your hair that smells like it." He Weimin could hear Li Yuanjun take a deep breath and sigh.

He Weimin pondered what Li Yuanjun might mean, but it seemed to be getting harder and harder to concentrate. "I added some herbs to the water. Maybe it's their scent you mean," he finally came up with a solution.

"Hm, herbs, flowers, and the other green stuff. You like testing new smells and flavors," Li Yuanjun said.

"Yes, my work in the pharmacy gives me the opportunity to do that. Since I became blind, my sense of smell and taste have become very important to me."

"That makes sense, but you also seem to have a talent for it. You'll be a good successor to Deng Tingfeng one day."

"What do you mean?" He Weimin asked, who didn't understand what Li Yuanjun was getting at.

"Well, Deng Tingfeng always says that the ceiling is falling on his head, and he misses traveling. I think he's planning to train you as his successor so that he can resume his research trips in peace and quiet to look for new recipes and ingredients." After a short pause, Li Yuanjun added, "However, you would have to stay at the Yaosen for that."

"I guess I would have to," He Weimin said simply but didn't dare to ask whether Li Yuanjun could imagine a life together with him. It was all still too new for He Weimin, who had believed until yesterday that Li Yuanjun would never return his feelings.

To distract Li Yuanjun from the topic, He Weimin grabbed Li Yuanjun's collar to pull him in for a kiss. An imprecise but proven method, as he had discovered. On his second attempt, he found Li Yuanjun's mouth invitingly open and slid his tongue into it.

Li Yuanjun had not been lying when he had claimed to be adaptable. Although he liked to take the initiative, he was also prepared to relinquish the lead and receive attention himself. He Weimin's observation was confirmed by a soft whimper that Li Yuanjun let out when he bumped into his tongue.

He Weimin didn't know how much time had passed when he felt a few drops hit his face. After weeks without rain, the summer suddenly decided that today was the time to make up for all the precipitation.

"It is raining," He Weimin tried to make Li Yuanjun aware of their dilemma.

"You can always use rain," Li Yuanjun mumbled absent-mindedly. He did not allow himself to be disturbed in his activity, which consisted of exposing more of He Weimin's skin from under his clothes.

"It's going to rain heavily soon," He Weimin tried again. "Maybe we should go somewhere drier."

Li Yuanjun raised his head and seemed to finally notice that they were standing in the rain. "We need to get out of the rain quickly," he said, releasing his grip on He Weimin with a regretful sigh. In his eagerness, he grabbed the sleeve of He Weimin's coat to pull it along with him. He Weimin barely managed to slow Li Yuanjun down before they both involuntarily landed in the bushes.

After He Weimin reminded Li Yuanjun to collect their swords, they quickly left the clearing, hooked at the elbows. He Weimin no longer needed this kind of help, but the physical contact was too pleasant to give up voluntarily.

As they approached the Yaosen compound, Li Yuanjun asked, "What should we do? I can walk you home, but my house is closer."

He Weimin assumed that Li Yuanjun wanted to know whether they should call it a day or continue on. He thought about who, or rather what was waiting for him at home, which made it easier for him to answer.

"I think I'd like to get to know your home," He Weimin replied.

Li Yuanjun responded to He Weimin's answer by increasing their pace.

The path to Li Yuanjun's house was not far, just as nothing seemed to be far from each other on the school grounds. Completely soaked by the rain but still giggling like two schoolboys, they reached Li Yuanjun's house. He Weimin couldn't remember ever laughing as much in his life as he did in Li Yuanjun's presence.

He Weimin could hear Li Yuanjun fiddling with the front door before half-pulling, half-carrying him over the threshold. "We need to get you out of those wet clothes right away before you catch a cold. And then off to bed to warm up," Li Yuanjun said, closing the door behind them.

"I was hoping you would at least offer me some tea before we end up in bed," He Weimin said as seriously as he could.

"Weimin, this is not what I meant," Li Yuanjun stuttered, only now realizing how his words must have sounded. "Can I offer you some refreshment or rather something to warm you up?"

"No need," He Weimin managed to say before the laughter he had been struggling to hold back burst out of him.

Li Yuanjun relaxed noticeably and rested his head on He Weimin's shoulder. "I can't think clearly around you. You're too much of a distraction," he admitted.

The admission pleased He Weimin. He was obviously not just one of many adventures for Li Yuanjun.

"Our swords are on a chest of drawers to your right. Now let's take off our coats and shoes, and then I'll describe the house to you," Li Yuanjun said, bending down to He Weimin's legs.

While He Weimin leaned on Li Yuanjun's shoulders, Li Yuanjun slipped off his shoes and put them down silently. A plop revealed that he was less careful with his own footwear. He Weimin handed Li Yuanjun his damp coat.

Li Yuanjun grabbed He Weimin's elbow. "Straight ahead is the living room with a table in the center and two armchairs. To the left, behind a curtain, is the kitchen. To reach the bedroom, we have to cross the living room. To the left of the bedroom is another small room that I use as a storeroom."

Li Yuanjun led He Weimin into the bedroom, repeatedly dodging things that had accumulated on the floor. At the entrance to the bedroom, He Weimin bumped his foot against what turned out to be a pile of unwashed laundry. "I have hardly got round to tidying up lately," Li Yuanjun justified himself. "You've distracted me too much."

He Weimin interrupted Li Yuanjun's attempt to explain with a kiss that landed on his cheek. He took a deep breath and mustered all his courage. "We don't want to catch a cold. Describe the bedroom to me, and then get out of those wet clothes."

In response, Li Yuanjun grabbed He Weimin's arm and pulled him along until they both landed next to each other on an unmade bed. "This is the bed," Li Yuanjun said unnecessarily before leaning toward He Weimin to give him a kiss on the mouth. "I'll take off my shirt before the bed gets wet," he said, and He Weimin noticed from the movement of the mattress that he did as he said.

He Weimin grabbed Li Yuanjun's bare arms and rolled awkwardly on top of him. He especially missed his eyesight in situations like this. He wasn't able to recognize Li Yuanjun's facial features to interpret his feelings.

Li Yuanjun stroked along He Weimin's arm. "Do you want to take off your shirt, too?" he asked.

He Weimin hesitated only briefly before removing his shirt. He was now sitting on Li Yuanjun in just his underwear and light summer trousers.

Li Yuanjun ran a finger along the waistband of He Weimin's trousers over his skin. "Hm, so soft," he murmured. "Can I switch on a light so I can see you better?"

"Is it that dark here?"

"The rain has caused dusk to fall earlier, and my bedroom only has a small window," said Li Yuanjun.

"Did you walk through your own house in the dark? Why didn't you switch on the light?"

"It wouldn't be fair if I could see you and you couldn't see me."

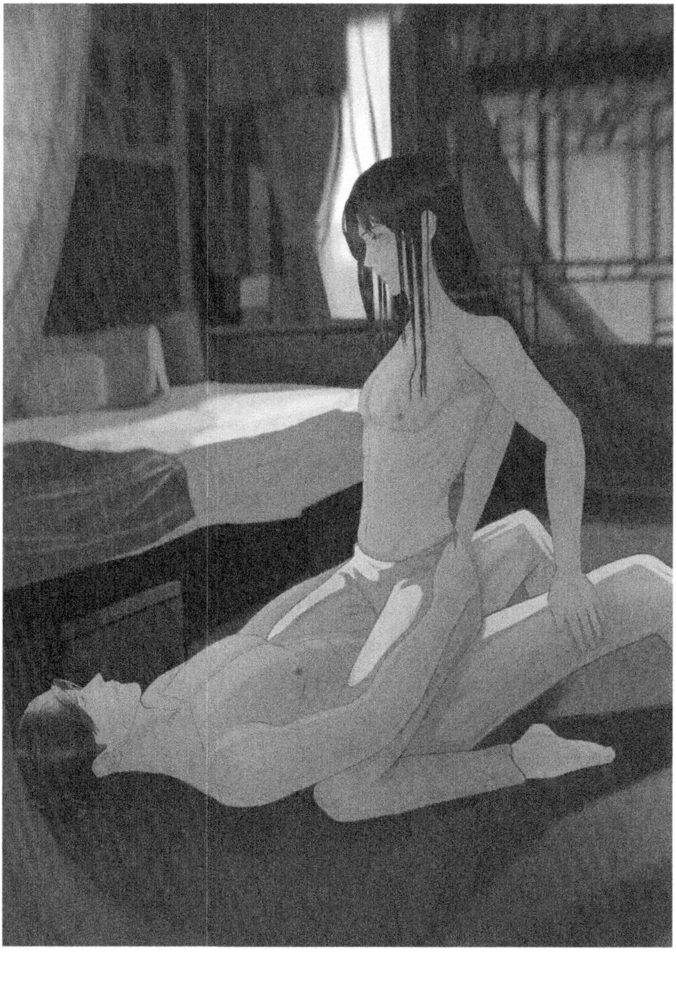

He Weimin had to laugh. "You're just impossible. Luckily, we didn't trip." With a wave of his hand, he ignited a small magical light and let it float toward the ceiling. "How's that?" he wanted to know.

"Better," Li Yuanjun said and tightened his grip on He Weimin's waist. "But you have to bend down toward me so that I can admire you properly."

Whoever had taught Li Yuanjun to lie so badly owed He Weimin eternal gratitude. He Weimin got involved in the game and slowly bent down to Li Yuanjun so as not to hurt him unintentionally. The movement caused Li Yuanjun's hands to land on He Weimin's buttocks. Big, strong hands, as expected of a swordsman.

He Weimin had probably paused in his movement for too long. "You know we won't do anything you don't want," Li Yuanjun tried to reassure him. "If you want, I'll stop right now and go out into the rain until my body understands."

"You don't have to catch a cold because of me," He Weimin said and gave Li Yuanjun a well-placed kiss on the lips. He was getting better and better at hitting Li Yuanjun's mouth.

"You really like kissing and being kissed," Li Yuanjun stated when He Weimin paused to take a deep breath. "Is there anything else you'd like to do?"

"Are you asking me if I'm still a virgin?" He Weimin tried to joke to distract himself from the fact that he was embarrassed.

"No, of course not. So, tell me."

"You're the worst liar I know," He Weimin blurted out.

"No, that's not true," Li Yuanjun contradicted him. "Compared to you, I'm a true virtuoso."

Before He Weimin could say anything in response, Li Yuanjun tightened his grip on him and rolled over with him until he was lying on top of him. "Got you. You can't run away now."

121

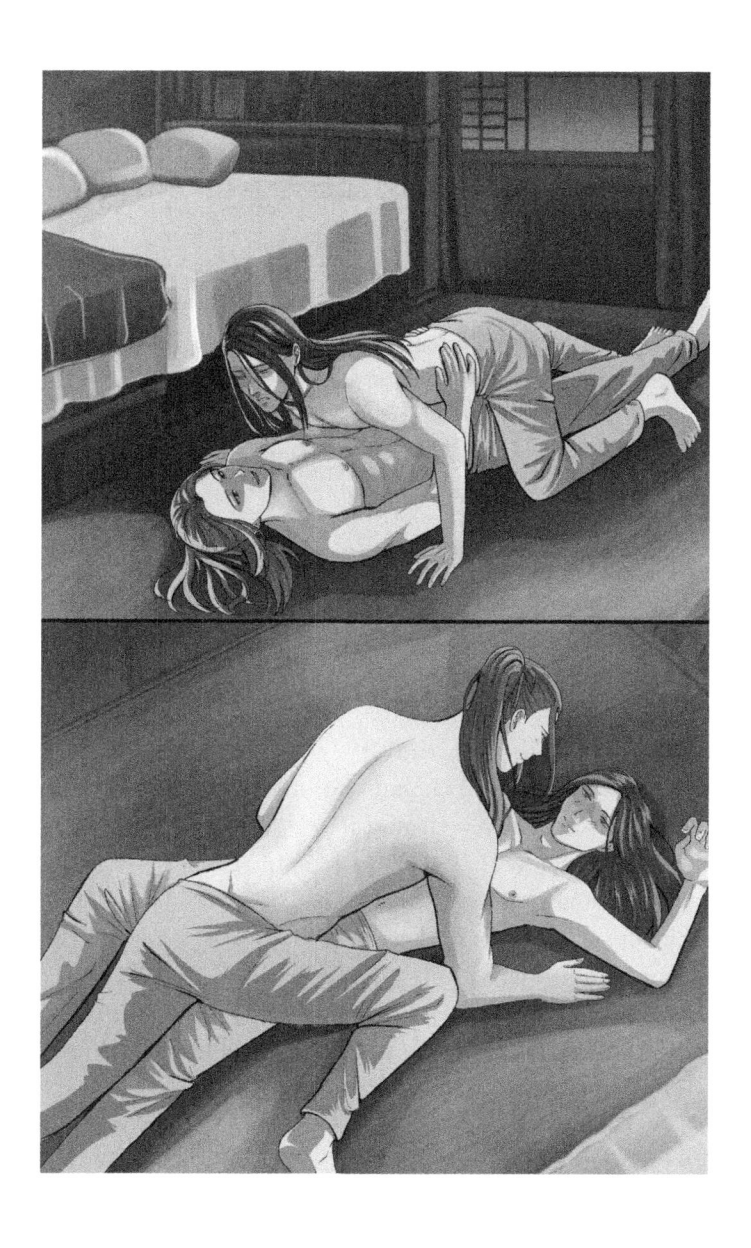

Li Yuanjun wouldn't let He Weimin forget his escape after the first kiss anytime soon. He still felt that Li Yuanjun was not pressing him into the mattress with all his weight. Li Yuanjun propped himself up with his elbows so that He Weimin could move his arms freely.

"There was a man from my clan with whom I had a relationship for several years," He Weimin hastened to say before his courage failed him. "We grew up together. After my uncle lost his hand and I spent more time at home again, we became a couple."

He Weimin resisted the urge to turn his face away from Li Yuanjun as he continued. "I didn't realize it at the time, but to him, I was just a substitute. I was only good enough for him when he couldn't find a mate."

Li Yuanjun took his time to reply. "If that's the case, then you weren't in a relationship. He was just taking advantage of you," he finally said.

"No, it wasn't like that," He Weimin disagreed. "We both had fun, even if he later pretended that there had never been anything between us after he got married."

"I understand," Li Yuanjun said in an emotionless voice. "What did you do that you enjoyed?"

Was that jealousy He Weimin heard in Li Yuanjun's voice? He decided that he must have imagined it. "He liked it when I used my mouth on him. I touched myself in the process, so we both got something out of it."

Li Yuanjun sank down on top of He Weimin and buried his face in his hair, which was spread out on the pillow. He Weimin felt Li Yuanjun take a few deep breaths.

"I assume you don't mean that you kissed," Li Yuanjun asked after he seemed to have calmed down.

"No, he didn't want that," said He Weimin, tilting his head slightly. He had only once dared to ask his lover for a kiss. He had vehemently refused his request, reasoning that such a thing was not done between men.

"Too bad for him. I was lucky enough to receive your first kiss. And hopefully many more." Li Yuanjun sealed his words with a kiss on He Weimin's forehead. He had obviously regained his good humor.

"I don't think we should use our mouths for anything other than kissing today," Li Yuanjun continued.

He Weimin was about to protest in disappointment when Li Yuanjun bumped into him with his lower body. "I didn't mean that's all we're going to do. We'll create new, pleasant memories for ourselves. We'll both get our money's worth in the process."

He Weimin was grateful that Li Yuanjun did the talking for them both. His lover bent down to whisper in He Weimin's ear, "Shall we take off some more clothes? I want to feel more of your bare skin."

In the past, He Weimin had always been clothed when he was with his lover. He had always regretted this. He ran his hands down Li Yuanjun's upper body with relish until he reached the waistband of his trousers. Like Li Yuanjun before him, he ran his hands along the waistband, making Li Yuanjun shudder. "Get rid of the clothes," He Weimin ordered.

Li Yuanjun expelled the air he must have been holding and rolled away from He Weimin. The rustling of the cloth showed He Weimin that Li Yuanjun was stripping off the rest of his clothes and carrying them next to the bed.

Before He Weimin could do the same, he had second thoughts. What would Li Yuanjun think of his body, which was covered in scars? One particularly large one from his last battle ran down his left leg. He thought about how Li Yuanjun had also kissed the part of his face that was covered in scars. They didn't seem to repel him.

He Weimin shook his head and took off his trousers and underwear in one motion. He sat up straight and exposed himself to Li Yuanjun's gaze.

124

When Li Yuanjun took a breath with a hiss, He Weimin knew that he could see everything. He reflexively wanted to cover the scars on his leg with his hands.

"Don't hide them," Li Yuanjun said, leaning in He Weimin's direction. "The scars represent what you've overcome. You can be proud of them."

Li Yuanjun first traced the scar with his finger before leaning down and spreading a few light kisses on the uneven skin. Before he reached the thigh, he paused and leaned back. "No," he admonished himself out loud, "it's just kissing today."

"You are one of a kind," He Weimin stated.

"I'm barely able to think straight. Besides, it's not fair that I have the advantage over you. I'm sure you want to *see* what you've got yourself in for."

He Weimin didn't know what Li Yuanjun meant at first until Li Yuanjun took his hand and placed it on his chest. "Now, you can look at me as much as you like."

He Weimin gladly accepted the invitation and ran his hand in light circles over Li Yuanjun's muscular torso. The fine hairs that grew there tickled He Weimin's palm. Most of the men He Weimin knew, including himself, didn't have much body hair. He decided he liked the feeling and was curious to learn how it would feel on other parts of his body.

He Weimin continued his exploration and ran his hand along Li Yuanjun's hip. As he slid lower, He Weimin could feel Li Yuanjun spreading his legs. He ignored the silent invitation and felt along one thigh. As he approached the hip area, the muscles twitched under his touch, and Li Yuanjun let out a low moan.

"Did you say something?" He Weimin wanted to know.

"No, take your time," came Li Yuanjun's reply in an unusually high-pitched voice that betrayed his tension.

He Weimin decided that he had stalled them both long enough. There would be time enough later to memorize Li Yuanjun's body shape. A tilt of his hand confirmed what he had already surmised. Li Yuanjun also had a generous amount of hair in the pubic area.

"Is it true that your hair is red all over?" He Weimin slipped out the embarrassing question in nervousness.

"So Tao and Long told you about this story?"

"They say you dropped your trousers in front of your classmates as a teenager to prove that your hair is red all over."

"It was all Long's fault," Li Yuanjun defended himself. "Because he has this fiery red dragon's mane, the others thought I had dyed my hair red to imitate him."

"And that's when you proved to them that you have red hair everywhere."

Li Yuanjun let out one of his laughs that He Weimin loved so much. "You should have seen the looks on their faces. They were definitely worth the month of kitchen duty Grandmother punished me with." He sighed, deep in his memories. "But it's true, it's all red. It's not the red of a flame, but rather a dark reddish-brown color."

"Reddish-brown, then," said He Weimin. "Now I can get a better picture of you." He felt his hand through the curls until he reached Li Yuanjun's erection.

A first, careful grip confirmed to him that Li Yuanjun already had to be as aroused as he was. A whimper from Li Yuanjun gave him the courage to run his fingertip along the shaft to memorize its shape. He Weimin rubbed the tip, on which a drop of fluid had formed, and used his other hand to stroke Li Yuanjun's testicles.

"I want to touch you, too," Li Yuanjun said in a rough voice.

Although He Weimin appreciated Li Yuanjun's assurance of his consent, his self-control also had its limits. He tightened his grip on Li Yuanjun's erection and urged him, "Go ahead! If I don't like something, I'll let you know. And the same goes for you, of course."

Li Yuanjun didn't need to be told twice and began to massage He Weimin's dick with practiced hand movements. He Weimin now put more force into his movements, which Li Yuanjun rewarded with a few uncontrolled hip thrusts and a loud moan. "That's good, keep going," he urged He Weimin.

Without He Weimin realizing it, Li Yuanjun had moved closer and closer to him until their knees were touching. "Spread your legs a little wider so that I can sit between them," Li Yuanjun urged him.

He Weimin didn't know what Li Yuanjun was up to, but he did as Li Yuanjun asked. After all, he had just insisted that Li Yuanjun did not ask his permission for every action. Li Yuanjun moved around on the bed and seemed to be rummaging around in a drawer, judging by the sounds.

Li Yuanjun sat facing He Weimin head-on so that their erections and testicles were touching. He Weimin was about to clasp them both with his hand and continue his massage when Li Yuanjun stopped him.

"Wait a minute. Let's make it a little more comfortable." Li Yuanjun started to spread a liquid over their erections.

It took He Weimin a while to recognize the smell. "Is that weapon oil?" he asked, trying not to flinch.

"Weapon oil?" Li Yuanjun seemed unimpressed by He Weimin's concern. "It's more of an all-purpose oil. Don't you know? It's sold in your pharmacy. I can assure you that it's absolutely harmless."

Deng Tingfeng had clearly told He Weimin that the tincture was weapon oil. However, he had already noticed that an unusually large number of customers who did not own weapons were asking for it.

Li Yuanjun hastened to reassure him. "We really do use the oil for a wide variety of purposes. Of course, you can use it to clean and grease your weapons, but you can also lubricate a squeaky door hinge. It works wonders on horses' hooves, and the baker swears that it helped her dog's ear infection."

"Deng Tingfeng was obviously having fun with me," He Weimin endeavored to explain.

"I wouldn't have thought the old curmudgeon capable of that," said Li Yuanjun. "He must have really taken you to his heart."

"I hope that didn't ruin the mood?" asked He Weimin, not quite sure what to do with his hands.

"Not at all," Li Yuanjun assured him. "It's not enough to put me off. The interruption was actually quite useful to calm down a bit, and the oil is nice and warm now." He reached for He Weimin's hands and wrapped them around their members with his. He Weimin had to admit to Li Yuanjun that the oil made the movements easier.

"You could add a fragrance to the oil. I'm sure some people would like that," Li Yuanjun murmured absentmindedly. He paused in his movements. "Ugh, now I can't get Deng Tingfeng's grumpy face out of my head."

He Weimin had to laugh despite the situation he was in, which earned him a long kiss from Li Yuanjun.

Their hands resumed the gliding motion, and it didn't take long for them to find a rhythm together.

Li Yuanjun let go of He Weimin's mouth, which He Weimin used to take a breath. However, he was unable to catch his breath as Li Yuanjun kissed his way to He Weimin's ear. Once there, he ran his tongue along the shell. When he blew against the sensitive skin, it sent a shiver straight to He Weimin's length.

To further tease He Weimin, Li Yuanjun began to whisper in his ear. "Is that good? I know more things that will please you."

He Weimin's reply was a whimper that sounded like a plea to his ears.

"I want to see the look on your face when you lie back on my bed while I ride you," Li Yuanjun continued. "What do you think of that?"

He Weimin had not missed Li Yuanjun's own reaction to the suggestion, namely a noticeable swelling of his erection. "If you react like you are now, then a lot," He Weimin stated with what was left of his mind.

Unconsciously, they had both increased the speed of their hands.

"You would also look good naked on your hands and knees in bed," Li Yuanjun continued. He released the grip of one of his oily hands and placed it on the back of He Weimin's neck. "I would kiss you here first." Li Yuanjun began to massage said spot to emphasize his words. "Then I'll slowly work my way around." His hand traveled in massaging movements over He Weimin's shoulder blades and spine and finally lay flat over the spot on his back where the spine ends.

"I would stay here until you stretch out greedily toward my tongue." He Weimin couldn't help himself and thrust his hips backward at this idea.

Li Yuanjun's breathing became heavier and heavier, proving that he was not as calm as his words made him believe. A single oily finger slid further and further along Weimin's tailbone between the cheeks of his buttocks. "My tongue keeps sliding down until . . ."

Li Yuanjun must have sensed that He Weimin was on the verge of an orgasm and had increased the pressure of his hand. Waves of pleasure washed over He Weimin, and he noticed with satisfaction that Li Yuanjun was following him after a few uncoordinated movements of his hands.

He Weimin felt the warmth of the semen running over his hands and stomach. As the tension in his muscles eased, he sank down onto the bed, exhausted.

Li Yuanjun bent down to give He Weimin a quick kiss on the mouth before getting off the bed. "Wait here. I'm going to get us something to clean up." Li Yuanjun disappeared into another room.

He Weimin took a deep breath and felt down his body with one hand. He was still feeling the after-effects of his climax and rubbed his stomach down to his dick and testicles, lost in thought. Unconsciously, he spread the semen that was stuck there, with the thought running through his mind, that this was how animals marked their territory.

Li Yuanjun chose this moment to return to the bedroom.

"Hey, don't go on without me."

He Weimin could imagine what a sight he must have made. He resisted the first impulse to pull the blanket over his lap and instead let his hand slide further down.

When he heard Li Yuanjun take a hissing breath through his nose, followed by the sound of something wet landing on the wooden floor, he knew he had done the right thing. He admitted to himself that it excited him to tease Li Yuanjun until he lost his self-control.

"You know," said He Weimin. "I haven't had a partner for a long time, but that doesn't mean I've been celibate."

This assertion was only partly true. Thanks to his roommates, he had hardly found an opportunity to satisfy himself in recent months.

"You have two beautiful, skillful hands," Li Yuanjun said. "Maybe one day you will show me what tricks you can do with them."

Li Yuanjun even managed to turn the embarrassing after into an exciting promise with a simple remark.

"The only feat I can manage today is to clean myself up before my hands get stuck," He Weimin said regretfully.

"It's really too bad that we're no longer teenagers," Li Yuanjun responded to He Weimin's joke.

"As we all know, quality trumps quantity, so get your grandfatherly ass over here and give me the promised cloth," He Weimin demanded, straightening up into a sitting position.

Li Yuanjun picked up the cloth he had dropped without saying a word and sat down on the mattress. With slow movements, he carefully cleaned He Weimin of the traces of their activity and then did the same for himself.

As the silence continued, He Weimin thought he had upset Li Yuanjun with his remark. The cloth landed on the floor again, and Li

Yuanjun began to speak. "I don't have the ass of a grandfather yet. If you want wrinkles, you'll have to stay with me for a long time."

He Weimin had to swallow hard before he replied in a raspy voice, "Is that what you want? To be with me?"

Li Yuanjun clasped He Weimin's hands with his. "For a very, very long time," he confirmed.

"And if I decide not to stay at the Yaosen, what will you do then?" He Weimin wanted to know, remembering Su Tao and Cai Long's words, that Li Yuanjun had never really been attached to his conquests.

"I will follow you, of course," Li Yuanjun replied, "but only if you let me," he added.

"But your family and friends . . ."

"They will still be there when we come to visit them. So, what, do we want to travel the world after we've been to your clan? Or do you want to go back to your family? You could introduce me as a good friend."

"Yes, I mean no," He Weimin stuttered. "I want to be with you for a very, very long time, but I don't want to travel the world. At least not for now. The Yaosen is the place where I want to stay and build a new life for myself. And as for my clan, while I will always remain a part of it, I will not return there for any length of time."

He Weimin had spoken without interruption before his courage could fail him and was now waiting with bated breath for Li Yuanjun's reaction.

He leaned toward He Weimin to catch him in a hug. "My grandmother was right, as always. You're the best thing that's happened to me, and I'll do everything I can to make sure we stay together."

"Mhmm," Li Yuanjun buried his face in He Weimin's hair, which had to look like a storm-tossed bird's nest, without seeming to be bothered by it. "Grandmother usually has a solution for everything.

So I'm surprised she hasn't thought of a suitable place for you to live yet," he thought aloud.

"I am content," He Weimin replied. "Xue Mengyao and Dai Liuxian are both very nice and have always supported me."

"They are," Li Yuanjun confirmed. "Still, it cannot be easy living in close quarters with a couple in love."

Li Yuanjun had hit the bull's eye with his guess. Perhaps He Weimin could spend more time with Li Yuanjun in the future to catch up on his lost sleep. Before he could express his thoughts, Li Yuanjun said, "I have the solution. Why don't we live together in my house? At least you'll have a bit more peace and quiet. If you want, you can set up the storeroom as your study. I will also try out or taste everything you make there."

He Weimin had strong doubts about the quietness part, but that wasn't a problem for him.

Without waiting for He Weimin's reply, Li Yuanjun continued with his explanation. "You could move in here tomorrow. I'm sure your roommates will be happy to help us move your things and the bed."

"I see, so we will be moving in together tomorrow," He Weimin simply replied.

"That's what couples usually do," explained Li Yuanjun, who had missed He Weimin's concerns.

"If that's the case, then we can do without a second bed when we move." He Weimin was aware that this would clearly show outsiders that they were lovers. He didn't want to be someone's secret again. How would Li Yuanjun react to his proposal?

"As always, you have the best ideas," Li Yuanjun agreed without hesitation. "That will make the move easier. And now it's time to sleep. We have a busy day ahead of us."

Li Yuanjun tightened his embrace around He Weimin and, pleased with himself, kissed him on the forehead. As they stretched out together in bed, He Weimin realized that they were still naked. He leaned over the edge of the bed and wanted to feel his undergarments.

"There will be enough time in the morning to find out which item of clothing belongs to whom. But I can gather up your clothes and hang them up if you like," said Li Yuanjun, who had misunderstood He Weimin's movement.

He Weimin sank back into bed, deep in thought. "That won't be necessary," he finally replied. "I think it is time for me to change my wardrobe. Maybe you could help me choose the colors of my clothes? I was thinking of something to match the Yaosen and you."

"We will have our own family colors," Li Yuanjun murmured sleepily and carefully spread the duvet over them. As Li Yuanjun snuggled close to He Weimin's back, he thought that sleeping naked could be quite comfortable.

When Li Yuanjun remained silent, He Weimin thought he had fallen asleep and closed his eyes to do the same. He remembered in time to switch off the magical light that was still slightly illuminating the room. As his thoughts slowly drifted off, Li Yuanjun began to speak again.

"You move so purposefully during training. Did my grandmother help you restore some of your vision?"

Li Yuanjun seemed to be one of those people who liked to talk themselves to sleep.

He Weimin replied without turning to Li Yuanjun. "No, I will never be able to see real pictures again. However, Li Xifeng's technique allows me to develop a rough idea of my surroundings by sending out energy pulses. You can think of it like the spots of light that appear when you rub your eyes. The brain has to learn to convert these flashes of light into something resembling an image."

Li Yuanjun used his arm, which had been resting loosely on He Weimin's waist, to pull him closer, regardless of the summer temperatures.

"So, I'm curious. How was it possible for you to recognize it was me at the clearing?"

He Weimin was glad that Li Yuanjun could not see his face, which was beginning to turn dark red. "You're not just a simple lightning bolt to me," he admitted. "You're more like one of those magical signals that can be seen for kilometers, like fireworks."

A laugh went through Li Yuanjun's whole body and made the mattress shake. "And yet you didn't notice when I snuck up on you on the way to the glade."

"I must have been distracted by Su Tao's talk of kisses. As distracted as I was at the time, I wouldn't even have noticed a horde of demons."

"I hope you don't mean the wine when you say kisses."

"No, and now go to sleep."

"Speaking of wine, I think we forgot the jugs at the glade."

"They will still be there tomorrow and were almost empty anyway."

"Your uncle," Li Yuanjun muttered.

"What does my uncle have to do with the wine now?"

"Nothing. But you still haven't told me how he died."

He Weimin was beginning to doubt that he would be able to sleep that night or any of the next nights. Perhaps it would be better to stay in his old accommodation and try earplugs after all?

"Just this one more question," Li Yuanjun begged, bumping his lower body against He Weimin's hip in invitation. "I can't fall asleep from excitement otherwise."

He Weimin knew what kind of excitement would soon prevent him from falling asleep if Li Yuanjun didn't stop soon. He Weimin had to find a way to get Li Yuanjun to sleep. He would try a new method.

"Who said my uncle was dead? I don't remember saying anything like that."

"But you said yourself that you took Sword from your uncle. How is that possible if he's still alive?" Li Yuanjun fell into He Weimin's trap as hoped.

"You know, it's a very long story. I'm far too tired today to tell it in full."

"You can't do that. Do you want me to tease the answer out of you? At least give your beloved a little hint."

"My beloved?" He Weimin repeated.

"Well, you know," Li Yuanjun mumbled meekly into He Weimin's neck. "Your dearest friend, partner, soul mate?"

He Weimin had struck a nerve. He decided that he could still pursue this matter later. Now was the time to put his beloved—a pleasant warmth spread through him at this word—to silent.

"All right, a tiny hint. But after that, it is time to sleep. And starting tomorrow, there'll be a part every evening to solve the mystery. Is that a deal?"

"Yes, my cruel soul mate."

He Weimin could hardly believe that he had just declared himself a storyteller for a grown man. But what wouldn't you do for a few hours of peaceful sleep? He thought about where to start and then decided on the most obvious one.

"I don't remember claiming that my uncle is still alive, either."

Happy Ending

Glossary

Cultivation/cultivating

Cultivation is when a character practices a form of magic in order to become stronger (longevity, special techniques, etc.). This **cultivation** is achieved through meditation, for example, by absorbing energy from the environment. The level of **cultivation** can also be increased by obtaining/using an artifact (weapon, piece of jewelry, etc.).

Clan/sect/school

Cultivators who do not act autonomously (or in pairs/small groups) usually belong to a **clan**, **sect**, or **school**. The differences between these are not clearly defined, and there is some overlap.

Clan, **sect,** or **school** describes a group of people who have united around a common cause or belief.

The term **clan** is often used when the members are related to each other by blood. This is not the case with a **sect**.

The term **school** is used less frequently and is not identical to a modern educational institution exclusively for adolescents. The philosophical schools of ancient Greece (e.g., the Stoa) come quite close to the concept. A person can spend a period of time (months/years) as a guest student or guest cultivator in such a **school** and still remain a member of their own **clan** or **sect**.

Magic swords & swordplay

Cultivators are able to use their **swords** as a means of transport. To do this, they stand on the broadside of the sword blade.

Depending on their cultivation level, cultivators can send their sword flying in any direction by signaling with their hand. The sword can fight for them in this way and flies back into their hand on command. A **sword** can also be used to send out energy waves.

Wedding/wedding ritual

One part of the wedding ceremony is the couple's walk to their new home. In this tradition, it is customary for the bride to be veiled. As the veil is usually opaque, she cannot see anything and must be led by the groom.

Red is the symbolic color of weddings and stands for luck and prosperity.

Coughing/spitting blood

A person who spits blood is either sick, wounded, or mentally disturbed. Internal injuries or injuries, in general, are not a prerequisite for the phenomenon.

Characters

Li Yuanjun

Li Yuanjun is Li Meifen's son. After the death of his mother, he was raised by his grandmother, Li Xifeng, the matriarch of the Yaosen. Su Tao is not only his adoptive brother, but also one of his best friends. Li Yuanjun teaches swordplay to the Yaosen students.

He Weimin

He Weimin is a member of the Ningjinghui clan. After he was seriously wounded in battle about a year ago and lost his vision, he joined the Yaosen as a guest member. He Weimin works in the Yaosen pharmacy as an assistant to the alchemist Deng Tingfeng.

Su Tao

Su Tao was abandoned by his parents near the Yaosen at the age of six. After being adopted by Li Meifen, he developed a deep friendship with his adoptive brother Li Yuanjun and works as a teacher at the Yaosen.

Cai Long

A half-dragon who works as a blacksmith for the Yaosen.

Xue Mengyao

Senior student of the Yaosen. Roommate of He Weimin.

Dai Liuxian

Senior student of the Yaosen. Roommate of He Weimin.

Li Xifeng

Founder and matriarch of the Yaosen School for Cultivators. Her exact age is unknown, but tales of her existence go back more than 300 years. Li Xifeng has no biological children but has a number of adopted children, including Li Meifen. After Li Meifen's death, she took over the upbringing of her grandsons, Li Yuanjun and Su Tao.

Deng Tingfeng

An alchemist who runs the Yaosen pharmacy.

Lai Meixiu

A young woman whose parents own the Blue Pearl, the Yaosen's inn.

Lai Enlai

Infant. The youngest child of the Lai family. Brother of Lai Meixiu.

Wan Zemin

Yaosen healer who often forget the time while collecting herbs.

Hao Wenling

Hao Wenling is a member of the Ningjinghui clan, to which He Weimin also belongs.

He Wenyan

He Wenyan is He Weimin's father and a member of the Ningjinghui clan.

He Ru

Son of He Wenyan. He Weimin's youngest brother and a member of the Ningjinghui clan.

Luo Huiliang

Uncle of He Weimin on his mother's side.

Ticulgubh

A water god.

Smaq

Son of the water god Ticulgubh and twin brother of Kniq.

Kniq

Son of the water god Ticulgubh and twin brother of Smaq.

Acknowledgments

Thank you for giving *Yaosen: The Kiss* a try.

I really hope you enjoyed it and had a pleasant time reading it. I'd be grateful if you could leave a review where you bought it or wherever you like.

"When self-publishing, you handle everything by yourself and are on your own."

Who is claiming such nonsense? I certainly had a lot of kind helpers who accompanied me on the way to publication:

Alia, who pointed out to me that the smithy should be outside the building.

Andy, who didn't despair at the commas I put in with the grit box. Hooray for the comma king!

Jas, your comments made me realize that the wrong bride has worn the veil.

MyFairy, you live up to your name. Thanks to you, I've learned everything there is to consider when designing a book cover.

Fluffydumplin, your "alrighty!" has motivated me to do my very best.

Irul, thanks to you, I learned a lot about the different shades of red hair.

Hatzumomo, your talent never ceases to amaze me.

Surya Dexter, thank you for making He Weimin a man (you get my point).

All those who worked so hard on the English translation: **Max, Ami, TJ, Jen, Mel, Michael, Isabel, Paige, Adele.**

A big thank you to each one of you!

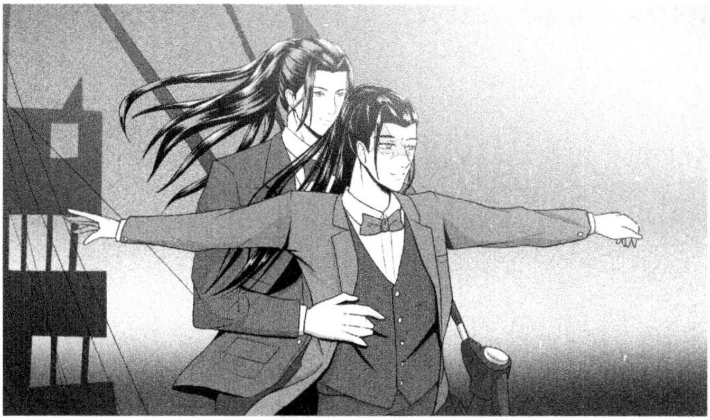

About the author

Illustration: © senviz

Nancy's family is sure that she raised herself with JRPGs and novels.

Her first experience with the genre of M/M Romance in 2017 was love at first sight. When she ran out of books to read, she decided to write her own stories.

When Nancy isn't working on her next book, she pays homage to her garden's harvest goddess and dedicates herself to her animal entourage.

Information on new releases will be announced on the Goodreads blog: goodreads.com/Nancy_Richter.

Follow Nancy on her Amazon author page: amazon.com/author/nancy-richter to stay up to date.